Why did Coop have to bring sex into the equation?

Violet had been so happy as an undersexed, obsessively committed federal agent, thinking about nothing but busting bad guys.... Now this stakeout with Coop changed everything. They were even in the *honeymoon* suite, for heaven's sake!

Coop peeled off his shirt in one easy motion, revealing an absolutely gorgeous torso, all gleaming skin and hard muscle. Mouthwatering. His hands went to the top button on his jeans.

She held her breath.

The rivet snapped, the zipper rasped and his jeans slipped all the way to the floor. He kicked them off, standing there in nothing but a pair of tighty whities. She could see the long hard ridge under the front flap, and hoped she wouldn't faint.

She moved closer, reaching for him, dying to touch him, but he backed away with a grin.

"Your turn... Take it off, Violet," he urged, his heated gaze never leaving her.

It was time to make up her mind. Pull away, say no and huddle with her gun and her badge and her wiretaps? Or hang on, say yes and tumble into ecstasy with Coop?

"Yes," she whispered. *"Yes."* And she pulled her T-shirt off over her head and threw it away.

Dear Reader,

I can't believe we're finally here at *Packing Heat,* book three of my TRUE BLUE CALHOUNS miniseries. I hope you've enjoyed playing around with these dynamic Chicago cops as much as I have.

Cooper is the third of three boys, the baby of the family, the one his brothers think is a bit of a goofball. Whereas Jake relies on logic and Sean relies on intuition, Cooper gets by on charm. Although that isn't really my style (I'm more of a mix of logic and intuition), I can certainly relate to Cooper. As the third of three daughters, I know what it's like to be the baby of the family. Yes, you get a lot of perks and maybe a little spoiled, but no one takes you very seriously!

That's why I gave Cooper a heroine like FBI agent Violet, who is smart and serious and a little reserved. I thought Cooper's charm would melt her, while the challenge she presented would bring out the tiger in him. They definitely brought out the heat in each other.

It's been fun wrapping up THE TRUE BLUE CALHOUNS, partially because of Cooper and Violet, and partially because of the nature of their story. It's a romp. A sexy romp, but a romp nonetheless. I hope you enjoyed the ride!

Best wishes,

Julie Kistler

Books by Julie Kistler

HARLEQUIN TEMPTATION
907—MORE NAUGHTY THAN NICE
957—HOT PROSPECT *
961—CUT TO THE CHASE *

*The True Blue Calhouns

JULIE KISTLER

PACKING HEAT

To Nancy —
See you in October,
sweetie!
Julie Kistler

HARLEQUIN®

TORONTO • NEW YORK • LONDON
AMSTERDAM • PARIS • SYDNEY • HAMBURG
STOCKHOLM • ATHENS • TOKYO • MILAN • MADRID
PRAGUE • WARSAW • BUDAPEST • AUCKLAND

To Birgit, the perfect editor.
Thank you so much!

ISBN 0-373-69165-3

PACKING HEAT

Visit us at www.eHarlequin.com

Printed in U.S.A.

_____Prologue_____

SOMETHING WAS UP. Cooper Calhoun had no doubt about that.

He stretched out his legs on the Adirondack chair, settling his hands behind his head as he contemplated his next move. It was just fine sitting in the shade next to the fishing cabin, watching the morning sun dapple the calm blue water of the lake. But that didn't mean he was completely in the dark.

Something was up.

Oh, sure, his brothers and his parents all dismissed him as the family goofball, the clueless, irresponsible one. But they were wrong. Cooper knew very well that if he was at the fishing cabin all by himself, more than twelve hours after his two older brothers should've been there, that some new Calhoun family plot had been hatched, altering everybody's plans, and nobody had bothered to tell him.

"Par for the course," Coop grumbled, unwinding enough to pitch a rock into the lake. He ought to be used to it by now. "How long do they expect me to wait here just on the off chance they might show up?"

He didn't even like fishing. So what was he doing here? Brother bonding trip. Yeah, right. Hard to do any bonding when you were the only brother in attendance.

As the youngest and least illustrious of the True Blue Calhouns, that extremely illustrious family of Chicago police officers, he'd been living with this state of affairs for a long, long time. Dad was a career cop, a Deputy Superintendent in line to be First Deputy. Jake, brother number one, had followed all the rules and dotted all the *is* and climbed the ladder one careful rung at a time. Now a sergeant, he'd done very well for himself with his methodical approach to life. Sean, brother number two, took his own, more intuitive path, but he'd earned himself a meritorious promotion to detective with his amazing ability to cut through artifice and spot liars and felons from fifty miles away.

Compared to them, Cooper was a piker. No one took him seriously, not when he was still a rookie who thought there ought to be more fun in life than merely being True Blue. Hey, why couldn't you have both? What was so wrong about that?

Straightening, Cooper lifted himself enough to get his cell phone out of his pants pocket to check for messages one more time. Since there was no phone at the cabin, the cell should've been the best way to go if his brothers had needed to reach him. Cooper frowned at the silver gadget in his hand. Battery was running low. Plus there wasn't much of a signal, not enough to call out, and there hadn't been since he'd reached the cabin.

Hmm... No signal. Would that stop messages from getting in, too? That hadn't occurred to him, but it suddenly sounded like the logical conclusion. It was actually kind of a cheerful thought. If it was just a mechanical thing, modern technology letting him down, Cooper would feel a whole lot less left out.

Rousing himself from the lounge chair, he went back inside for his keys. He didn't want to go all the way back to Chicago to find out what the heck the story was, but maybe he could drive in the direction of civilization, until he got close enough to a satellite tower to connect with his voice mail or get a call out to one brother or the other. It was better than lounging around doing nothing.

With his key in hand, Cooper jumped into his Jeep, plugged in the phone to at least charge up the battery, and started to drive away from the lake. He checked every few minutes, but there was still no signal.

He shook the phone, as if that might help. He held it out the window. Still no go. It took a good half hour and a stop at a bait and tackle shop on the top of a rolling hill before the phone managed to scrounge up even one little bar, the kind that appeared in the corner to tell him he could finally contact the outside world. And when the bars finally consented to multiply, the number 2 popped up in the bottom corner of the display. Meaning he had two messages. Two brothers, two messages. Didn't have to be a detective to figure that one out.

Cooper punched in the code to play them back. He could barely hear Jake's voice, from sometime yesterday afternoon, mumbling about handling some crisis for Dad and not being able to come. Timed about two hours later, the other message came in a little stronger.

"Hey, Coop, it's Sean. I'm tied up. Jake says he's off on a mission for Dad, and Mom is giving me grief about something else. You can go ahead to the cabin if you want," his middle brother's voice instructed through a bunch of static, "and I'll try to meet you there later."

Yeah, well, that was from yesterday, too, and Sean was nowhere to be seen today. It seemed as if *later* had turned into *not at all*.

"Thanks, bro," Cooper said darkly, shoving the phone back into its holder. Mom giving him grief about something, huh? Cooper knew his brother well enough to know that Sean didn't do anything he didn't want to. "Giving him grief" in Sean-speak meant she'd talked him into some mission, too, and he thought it was a better deal than fishing with Cooper, as long as Jake wasn't coming, either.

So they'd both taken off rather than meet him at the cabin—Jake on a secret assignment for their father and Sean on one for their mother—and neither was coming. It seemed like an incredible coincidence that both parents would cook up emergency errands just when the boys were heading out of town. Sean could say that his assignment wasn't related to Jake's, but Cooper had serious doubts that was true. If he knew his parents, they would be heading for the same target from different sides, pitting their favorite sons against each other. Of course, at the moment Coop had no idea what that target could be.

But one thing was for sure. When something interesting was happening in the Calhoun family, nobody trusted Cooper to do squat.

Heading back toward the cabin, he stewed. He was supposed to be on vacation for two weeks, so his schedule was wide open. Should he stay and drink beer and fish, all by himself, waiting for brothers who might never deign to show up? Forget them and have a good time, anyway? Or head back to the city, to find out what was really going on?

As he pulled back onto the dirt road leading to the cabin, Cooper made up his mind. He was tired of being the easygoing, adaptable, overlooked one in the family. Time to step up and prove a few things.

He was going to throw his gear back into the duffel bag and close up the cabin ASAP. If Jake and Sean ever arrived, let them be the ones sitting around cooling their heels all alone in the woods.

"I'm going back home," he said out loud. "I'm going to figure out where the heck they went and what they're up to."

Mom thought Sean was the son with all the answers, and Dad thought Jake walked on water, but maybe they would have to change their tunes. If Cooper played the hero for once and solved this puzzle before anyone else, they would have to admit that he was as worthy of trust and respect as any other True Blue Calhoun.

Cooper smiled grimly. Yep. That was exactly what he was going to do. He would show them there was one more Calhoun to be reckoned with. And beat them at their own game.

1

IT WAS LATE by the time Coop got back to his house in Chicago, but he wasn't tired. He was still fueled by righteous indignation at being odd man out one more time. What was the deal, anyway? Why didn't anyone in his family trust him? Was it his fault he was born third?

"It's really unfair," he muttered as he tossed his duffel bag into the house.

After trying to reach both brothers and getting messages on their machines that they were out of town, Cooper tried his parents' house, to see if they could shed any light on where Jake and Sean had gone off to. But neither of them was in, either, and all this telephone tag only made him crankier.

He decided he needed to improve his mood, and there was no better way to do that than to join some friends from the station for a drink in a favorite Rush Street night spot. After all, it was Saturday night. But he was still brooding over the issue of being overlooked and underappreciated within the Calhoun family, and his pals noticed right away that Good Time Cooper had a dark cloud hanging over him.

"You're on vacay," one of them said, wandering over from the pool table. "Lighten up, will you?"

"Yeah, yeah. I'm lightening." He noticed a pretty brunette keeping a low profile over in the corner, and he wondered what she would do if he sent a drink over there. Long dark hair, pale skin, a certain don't-talk-to-me attitude he found entertaining. Yep. Definitely his type. And she was alone, too....

But before he'd even had a chance to take a step in that direction, some brassy redhead in tight jeans and an even tighter tube top sidled up on the other side and asked him to buy her a drink. "My name's Tonya," she said breathlessly. "What's yours?"

It was amazing he even saw her face, considering how tight her top was and how much cleavage was happening under there, but he played it safe and focused above the neck. Not bad looking, he decided, but too much makeup and not his type. He preferred classy brunettes, like the one there in the corner, and this woman was neither classy nor a brunette, at least not at the moment. Hard to tell what color she'd started out with, but that violent shade of red sure wasn't it. As he turned back to the bar, he signaled the bartender to give her the drink, anyway. It seemed polite.

But once she had her "Sex on the Beach" cocktail in hand, she practically draped herself over him and asked for his name again. "Come on, you know you want to play with me," she teased. "Tonya. C'mon. Say my name. Ton. Ya."

He could tell she thought she was being seductive, but he was definitely not interested. And the other one he was interested in was probably going to see him with this one and take a hike before he ever got to talk to her. Before he could get the words out of his mouth to tell the redhead he wasn't into her, however, some drunken lout gave him a shove from behind.

"Don't be messin' with my woman," the guy blustered. He was short, angry and bald, with a whole mess of tattoos on his muscular arms. Not exactly a great-looking guy, especially with that ugly expression on his face. Whether it was a case of too much to drink or steroid rage, Cooper wasn't interested in contending with him.

"Ooh, I love it when my men fight over me," the girl giggled, bouncing her tube top up and down, practically licking her lips.

"Give me a break," Cooper muttered, rising from his bar stool. He wasn't interested in this creep's "woman" anyway, and he sure wasn't getting into a bar fight with some tattooed Anger Boy half his size. "Back off, pal. I'm not interested."

But the idiot shoved him again. Sheesh. Talk about a run of bad luck. As Cooper stared down the drunken boyfriend, trying to decide if he was really going to have to punch him just to get rid of him, four or five of his friends appeared at his back.

"What's up, Coop?" one of them asked quietly. Trust his brothers in blue to provide backup.

Confronted with that wall of serious cop muscle, the redhead apparently decided flight was her best option. "We better leave, Joey," she said suddenly, grabbing her boyfriend's tattooed arm, backing away. "Come on." Cooper could see her mouth the word "*cops*" at him.

The boyfriend let himself be led away, but he kept muttering and flexing and spitting out dire threats in Coop's general direction the whole way. It was a pretty sad sight, and one of Cooper's friends started to laugh.

"When I told you to lighten up, I didn't expect you to pick a fight with some mope over the first girl who walked by," he said as he took the next stool. "Jeez, Coop. You usually have better taste than that."

"She came on to me and I was trying to tell her I wasn't interested when the boyfriend got into it. Totally not my fault," Cooper insisted. But they still all seemed to think it was funny, hooting and making cracks about the trashy redhead and her bantamweight boyfriend. To get them off the subject, Cooper joked, "Can I help it if I'm a chick magnet?"

That prompted some more good-natured ribbing, but he wasn't really listening. The disturbing part was that he'd only been back in the city for a few hours, and he was already teetering on the edge of trouble. If not a chick magnet, he was at least a trouble magnet. No wonder the True Blue Calhouns thought he was a screwup.

He ventured a glance toward the corner by the dart board, where the brunette had been sitting, but she was gone. Just his luck.

"Listen, guys," he said, his mood getting bleaker by the minute. "I'm gonna get out of here. I just drove back from Wisconsin, so I'm tired."

They protested, but he really didn't want to stick around. The way his luck was running, the front line of the Bears would come in drunk and disorderly in the next five minutes.

As quickly as he could manage, he paid his tab, left the bar and caught a train back home. And then he didn't waste any time falling into bed, happy to be home, happy to be alone. Or at least not with any of the Tonyas of the world. He also realized he much preferred the noise of the city to those damn crickets and owls up at the lake. Much easier to relax to the sound of rattling El trains and car horns, back where he belonged.

As he drifted off to sleep, Cooper reminded himself to get right on the Mystery of the Missing Brothers first thing in the morning.

But after sleeping late—one of the joys of vacation—he woke up to a phone call from his sergeant asking him to fill in and help out with a little community outreach in Millennium Park that afternoon.

"Sure, why not?" As long as the fishing trip had fallen through and he was back in town, anyway, he might as well make himself useful.

It wasn't until almost five that he got a chance to go poking around into his brothers' mysterious errands. Still in uniform, he tried both their homes and got the same old "out of town" messages. So he set out with a renewed sense of purpose. First stop—Dad's office.

Neither his father's secretary nor his assistant was around, so Cooper walked right in without any preliminaries. Even though it was Sunday afternoon, Deputy Superintendent Michael Calhoun was on the job, as expected. The old man was bucking for a promotion, and time behind the desk on the weekend looked good.

Cooper shook his head. He shouldn't be so cynical; Michael Calhoun just liked putting in long hours.

"Coop," his dad said, glancing up from the papers he was poring over. He didn't look exactly happy to see his youngest son. Just grim, worried and kind of fidgety. Shoving the papers into a folder—oddly enough, not a Chicago PD file, but a plain manila one—he muttered, "I thought you were on vacation."

Cooper was still trying to figure this thing out. Nothing ever threw his father. So why the anxious attitude? And what was going on with the non-regulation folder that he was trying to hide? "Yeah," Cooper said slowly, "I was supposed to meet Jake and Sean at the fishing cabin in Wisconsin. But they didn't show. You know anything about that?"

"Me?" Looking distinctly guilty, Deputy Superintendent Calhoun picked up the file and quickly shoved it into his desk drawer.

"Yeah. Jake left me a message that he had to stamp out some fire for you," Cooper noted, leaning against the bookcase, trying to look casual. "As far as I can tell, he's out of town. What was that all about?"

"Well..." His father hemmed and hawed for a while. "I needed something looked into on the down-low, so I sent Jake."

Cooper arched an eyebrow. "On the down-low, huh?" What, was Dad watching MTV now? Maybe that and too many lattes was what was making him so edgy. "Where'd you send him?"

"It's nothing big. Some, uh, property I'm thinking

of buying. I thought Jake could investigate for me.
But it's no biggie. Just a small matter I needed to be
handled quietly." He shrugged. "I knew Jake could
take care of it."

And I couldn't.... But Cooper abandoned that idea
to focus on the clue his dad had just dropped. Jake
had gone on a secret mission to look at...real estate?

This was getting freakier by the minute. What kind
of property could his father possibly want that Jake
and only Jake could investigate for him? What was
wrong with a Realtor? And why the secrecy? Cooper
wasn't buying this story, not for a minute.

"Dad, if there's something going on—" But he
didn't get a chance to finish that thought.

"Hey, Mike, you in?" somebody called from the
outer office. Cooper knew that creaky, gusty voice. It
was Vince, his dad's ex-assistant, who'd been retired
for years.

"Hang tight. I'll be right out," his father shouted
through the open door, rising immediately from the
desk.

"Is that Vince?" Cooper asked. "Why not ask him
in? I'd like to say hi."

"Nah, you know Vince," his father said hastily.
"He gets, uh, flustered around too many people. Plus
the chairs are more comfortable out there. He had a
hip replacement, you know, so he can't sit in the ones
in here. I'll just talk to him, see what he wants."

All that stuff about Vince getting flustered because
there were two people in the room or needing a better
chair than the perfectly cushy one in front of him
sounded fishy, too. Vince was a sweet guy, loyal to a

fault, but not exactly quick on the uptake. Cooper got the idea that his dad wanted to head his friend off at the pass, before he spilled anything he shouldn't in front of Cooper.

"I'll go talk to him," his father said again. More sternly, he added, "You wait here." He pointed to the visitor's chair, as if ordering Cooper to plant himself and remain planted.

"Sure." There was no point in arguing about it. Besides, if Dad ran off to meet Vince in the outer office, that would give Cooper a chance to scan the papers his father had hidden in the desk.

After giving his desk drawer a final nudge and waiting for the click that told him it was locked, Michael Calhoun marched around his son and out the door into the anteroom. He carefully closed the door behind him.

But his voice carried through the wooden panel. "Hey, Vince, what's up?" he offered with an extra helping of volume that Cooper knew was for his benefit. "Surprise, surprise. Wasn't expecting to see you, buddy. How ya been?"

All very hearty and totally fake. So far, Cooper knew his dad had acted very suspicious about a file folder, he'd sent Jake off on some mysterious investigation that almost certainly did not involve real estate, and Vince, the ex-assistant who was incredibly loyal if not terribly mobile, was involved in this strange conspiracy. Weirder and weirder by the minute.

After a quick check near the door to make sure Vince and his father were safely occupied, Cooper

skirted back around the desk. His dad might've made
sure the drawer was locked, but he apparently didn't
remember that Cooper had seen him unlock it a hundred times. One good thing about being the family
lightweight was that nobody really expected him to
notice what was right in front of his face, like the fact
that Dad hid the key to his desk in the White Sox mug
under the rubber bands. Yep. Right there.

Smiling to himself, Coop quietly unlocked and slid
open the drawer, easing out the file he wanted to see.
Hmm... At first glance, it appeared to be some kind of
dossier on a person named Toni, with scribbled notes
and Post-its about Vince performing various surveillance duties. That in itself was pretty ridiculous, considering the fact that Vince's eyesight was right up
there with Mr. Magoo the last time Cooper had seen
him, and he didn't get around very well, either, what
with the hip replacement and at least one bad knee.

But, hey, Vince had apparently followed the "subject" to the Red Sails Travel Agency, if Cooper was
reading the notes correctly, and overheard her pur-
chasing two tickets on something called the...Ex-
ploding Jury? No, wait. Those were *r*s. Maybe it was
Explorer's Journey. The handwriting was terrible.
But Explorer's Journey sounded more like something
a perp would buy a ticket for. And whatever it was, it
had left yesterday, if the date scrawled next to the
name meant anything.

Unless Cooper was completely missing the boat,
Dad wanted to find this "Toni" person and had sent
Jake after her, skulking around some kind of explo-
ration tour. But why? There was no clue in the rest of

the papers, except for a note penciled in the margin that looked like "Lonely Hearts Con," although that could also have been "Lovely Hearse Co." Neither helped a whole lot. At least he knew what a lonely hearts con was.

It was a classic racket, where a woman came on to some lonely guy, pretending to be into him for love, and then she either conned him into handing over a lot of cash, or she rifled his bank accounts when he wasn't looking. Could "Toni" have tried to take his dad in a lonely hearts con game? Cooper couldn't believe Deputy Superintendent Calhoun would be an easy mark for that kind of scam. Or that his mother wouldn't have noticed and put the kibosh on it at the speed of light. She was very up-tempo when it came to her husband's time and attention. If Dad were straying, Mom would be on it like white on rice. Nope, this still didn't make sense.

Cooper moved back to the door, opened it a crack and verified that his father and Vince still had their heads together. Their voices low, they were conversing very intently, with his dad doing most of the talking and Vince just nodding. Whatever they were conferring about, they were certainly paying no attention to him.

Returning to the desk, Cooper pulled out a few photos that had been clipped to the inside of the folder. They were the blurriest, lousiest pictures he'd ever seen, and he rolled the chair a little closer to the window in search of better light. But the photos still looked as if they'd been shot through the deep end of a swimming pool. He could tell they were of a man and a woman, maybe sitting on a park bench, but other than one clear shot of some nasty-looking feet tottering in plastic hooker shoes, and tight acid-washed jeans from the thighs down, all he could tell was that they were both wearing dark clothes, the woman might be blond and average height, and Vince was one hell of a rotten photographer.

The voices in the outer office grew louder, and Cooper thought he heard, "See you later, Mike" in Vince's muffled voice. As footsteps approached the door and the knob jiggled, Cooper swiftly put the file back the way it had been, edged the drawer shut until it clicked, and dropped the key back under the rubber bands. By the time his dad cleared the door, Coop was in the visitor's chair again, whistling and staring at the ceiling.

"How's Vince?" he asked cheerfully, turning to greet his father with the most nonchalant expression he could muster. "Everything okay?"

"Yeah, fine," his dad said curtly. "So...you need anything else, Coop?"

"Nope. I'm good. Just wondered where Jake was. But you answered that one."

"Right." His dad sat down behind the desk, tapping two fingers against the front edge. "Nothing for you to worry about. I explained that. So we're good then. 'Cause I've got some work to do, so..."

Cooper scrutinized his father's face, which was pretty impassive. "What about Sean? You don't know where he's gone off to, do you? Something for Mom?"

"Nope." Mike Calhoun grimaced. "If your

mother's behind it, I'll bet it's something to do with a woman she wants him to hook up with. I can just hear her telling the poor guy he couldn't go fishing because her friend Bebe's second cousin's kid needed a date for some stupid shindig. You know your mom. She's bound and determined to get Sean married off."

While that did fit his mother's usual M.O., and the message from Sean about her giving him grief, Cooper still didn't think that was it. He had no real reason for that belief, except a gut feeling. Maybe, like his older brother, he was developing a knack for sifting out the truth. "But his machine says he's out of town," he noted.

His dad shrugged again. "So it was an out-of-town date. I told ya, Coop, I don't know where he is. I'm not his keeper."

And that seemed to be all he was going to get out of his old man. With a quick "Okay, well, I'll see you later", Cooper retreated from the office, wondering what his next move should be. He could follow up on this Explorer's Journey thing, but if it had left yesterday, there wasn't a whole lot he could do about it. Tracking down Mom and trying to worm some answers out of her seemed to be the best bet. Maybe she wouldn't be as secretive as her husband.

But Cooper changed his mind when he got to the bank of elevators and saw Vince waiting there. Hmmm... A co-conspirator.

Vince was a lot more stooped over than the last time Cooper had seen him, probably when he'd retired seven or eight years ago, and his hair was completely white now. His glasses seemed to have gotten thicker, too. Good old Vince. A slow elevator had added a little serendipity to the mix, it seemed, and Cooper decided he might as well see what he could get out of the old ex-cop while he had him.

"Hey, Vince," he called out. "How are you doing? Haven't seen you in a long time."

"Jake?" Vince asked gruffly, peering at him through his thick lenses. "That you?"

Jake? Cooper didn't really think he and his brother looked that much alike; Jake was a dead ringer for their dad at age thirty. But Coop and Jake were both tall, their coloring was similar and they shared the same broad-shouldered, athletic build. Plus everybody always told them their voices sounded alike. So he supposed it shouldn't have been a surprise that Vince had apparently mistaken him for his brother, especially given the fact that Vince was blind as a bat and hadn't seen Cooper in years. More serendipity.

Cooper suffered a momentary twinge of guilt for lying to sweet old Vince, but he thought it was probably okay if he just let the erroneous conclusion that he was Jake hang there, uncorrected. That wasn't lying, was it?

"How are you?" he asked again, purposely keeping his tone low and terse, like no-nonsense Jake.

"Doin' okay. Hey, I thought you was going on that tour, that Explorer thing, looking for that Toni. You didn't find her, did you?" Vince frowned. "I was just talking to your dad and he didn't say nothing about you finding her. But you got a bead on that tour, right?"

"The, uh, Explorer's Journey," Cooper said, trying to sound nonchalant. "Yeah, I'm on top of it."

"You found her?"

"Uh, no, not yet. I just came by to verify some details. You know, on the, uh, investigation." Okay, so now he was stepping over the line into actual lying. And doing a pretty lousy job of it, too, with all the verbal stumbling. "I was looking for a little more info. What have you got, Vince?"

"Nothing that I didn't put in my notes," he said quickly. "I only saw her from pretty far off. Your dad was sitting right next to her. What did he say?"

Dad was right next to her? Ah. The man in the blurry photos. Vince was letting slip a whole lot of details that were proving to be useful in filling in some of the blanks.

The elevator arrived, and Cooper held open the door, allowing Vince to shuffle in first. They were probably better off in the elevator than standing in the hall, where his father could catch him interrogating the old guy. "So what do you think her game is? Lonely hearts? Something else?"

"No, it was straight blackmail, as far as I know."

Blackmail? That was a new wrinkle. Who was she blackmailing? For what?

Vince shook his head. "It's a real shame when someone like her tries to cause trouble for a man as fine as Mike Calhoun, that's all I have to say."

Blackmailing *Dad*? Cooper's mind whirled. "Yeah, a real shame," he managed to murmur.

As the doors dinged open and Vince slowly walked out on the ground floor, Cooper followed, trying to figure out how to ask questions and get to the heart of this without giving away that he didn't know anything. He didn't need to worry. Vince was ready to talk.

"I want you to know, Jake, I didn't believe her, not even for a minute." Vince leaned close and kept his voice low. "Your dad was not cheating on your mom back in the seventies, and that girl is not his daughter. No way, no how. I hope you're not thinking that he did, 'cause he didn't. He wouldn't. I would stake my life on that."

Cooper was trying not to choke on this new information. What in the world? The blackmail was tied to allegations of Dad cheating on Mom? And maybe an illegitimate daughter?

"No, siree," Vince continued sadly, shaking his head. "No way the Mike Calhoun I know had, you know, relations with a hooker or fathered her kid."

Hooker? This just kept getting worse. Cooper took a deep breath. No wonder his dad was freaking out and sending Vince and Jake on harebrained searches. Cooper ran the whole crazy concept through his mind one more time. Could he possibly have misheard? Had he just landed on Mars?

Unless he was nuts, Vince had just said that this Toni woman was trying to shake down his father, claiming to be his illegitimate daughter from some liaison with a prostitute in the seventies.

But that was insane. Michael Calhoun was the straightest of straight arrows. He couldn't possibly have...

Not that it mattered. Mom would literally take him

apart limb from limb if she ever caught wind of this. Even without one word of truth to Toni's blackmail scheme—and Cooper had no doubt it was all a lie, it just had to be—the big promotion his father was so proud of would vanish, the papers would be full of horrible PR and Mom would have the entire extended family, not to mention anyone they'd ever met, in an uproar to end all uproars.

There was a potential family scandal of epic proportions looming on the horizon, and no one had said a word to Cooper.

"This is just...wrong," he muttered. "Wrong on so many levels."

"I know." Vince heaved a big sigh. "Well, we're all doin' what we can for him. I know I didn't mind pitching in. But you gotta find her on the double, Jake, and make sure she don't cause no more trouble."

"Yeah. I'm, uh, on it."

Cooper felt as if he were in a daze. He wanted to ask a whole lot more questions, but didn't dare. Seriously...some strange woman was claiming that *his* father, Deputy Superintendent Michael Calhoun, was *her* father, too?

Illegitimate daughters, hookers, infidelity and blackmail. Cooper was suddenly very sorry he had ever decided to look into this mess.

2

HIS NEXT STOP HAD TO BE his mother. What did she know about all of this? How bad was the fallout?

But when Cooper got to the family home in Beverly, he found a fairly subdued scene, and not at all what he expected. His mother and her friend Bebe, a hairdresser with a real flair for over-the-top style, were lounging around watching an old movie and eating popcorn. In the living room. He could smell the popcorn and hear the sound track of the movie the minute he walked in the door.

"Bebe, pause the DVD," Yvonne Calhoun called behind her as she answered the door. "I said *pause it*, hon. There must be a button on that remote."

As she turned to greet Cooper in the vestibule, she swiped a tissue over the smudged mascara under her eyes, which was also a new thing as far as Cooper was concerned. She was usually pretty immaculate with both her living room and her makeup.

Leaning closer, taking his arm, she confided, "Bebe and I were watching *An Affair to Remember*. It always makes me cry."

"Okay," he said doubtfully. His mother crying and allowing food in the living room, not to mention Bebe over on Sunday night watching a sad movie, all added up to suspicious behavior. Not the kind of apocalyptic blowout he'd expect if she knew about this blackmail and illegitimate daughter thing, but not an ordinary night for Mom, either. Who knew she even had a DVD player?

"Hon, I thought you were on vacation, or I would've asked if you wanted to come over for Sunday dinner," she told him as she led him toward the living room.

"Yeah, the fishing thing fell through. Jake and Sean didn't show."

"All right, well, as long as you're here, come and visit with Bebe and me. Sweetie, do you want some popcorn? Maybe a cookie?" she offered. "Did I tell you that Karen Hocksteider's new son-in-law has a sister? A lawyer. I could've asked her over for Sunday dinner, too, if I'd known you were free."

Cookie crumbs and buttery popcorn in the living room? And trying to match *him* up? Definitely weird. "You sure you don't want her for Sean?"

"No, he needs something different. He needs a homebody. But this one is a very practical, centered career girl with a good income," she added. "Just what you need to keep you on the straight and narrow."

"Ma, I'm always on the straight and narrow. I'm a cop," he reminded her.

"Not nearly as straight and narrow as you could be." Shaking her head sadly, she heaved a big sigh. Her voice was full of gloom when she said, "Just because you're a cop doesn't mean anything when it comes to behaving yourself."

This was a new tune for her. She had frequently taken issue with the fact that he dated around and never had one girlfriend for longer than a few months, but still... Usually, she just told him he was young and had time, while she concentrated her matchmaking efforts on Sean. But now... Confused, Cooper asked, "So you're saying you think I should act more like Dad and Jake?"

"Your father? Ha! I certainly hope not," she said darkly.

He was really at sea here. Did she know about the blackmail or not? This didn't seem like the right reaction either way. "I don't get it."

"Darling," she ventured, patting his cheek, "you can act like whoever you want. Your father, Jake, Sean...who cares? You're all the same. You're all men. Forget I told you about Karen Hocksteider's son-in-law's sister. You'd just break her heart."

"I would? Why?" He still didn't really grasp what she meant.

But she waved off his questions. "Come into the living room, sweetie. See Bebe. You can watch the movie with us."

"So where is Sean?" he persisted, trying to get back to something he could deal with. He was here to find out where she'd sent Sean, after all, and how that was related to his dad and Jake and the mysterious Explorer's Journey mission. "You didn't send him out of town on a fix-up, did you?"

His mother sent him a skeptical glance. "Heavens, no. Why would I do that?"

"So where did he go, then? I thought he said it was some errand for you."

"Nothing for you to worry about, Cooper. Sean will handle it." She reached up to pinch his cheek, making him feel about six. "You sit down and talk to Bebe, okay? I'll make some more popcorn."

"Ma, I don't want any—" But it was too late. She was off in search of popcorn whether he wanted it or not. He still couldn't get over the fact that she was passing out buttered snacks in the living room. And they had apparently been eating it on the floor, if Bebe and the big bowl next to her were any indication.

"Hi, sweetie," Bebe said from her place down there on the carpet, giving him a wave. "Look at you, so cute in your uniform. Makes your eyes look blue, doesn't it?"

"Yeah, I guess." Everybody said that.

Bebe's hair was sort of maroon today, and she had jiggly little butterflies attached in the front, like hair clips or combs or something. But her eyes were round and sparkling, and she was biting her lip, as if to hold back whatever secrets were bubbling inside her. Uh-oh. Whatever Mom knew, Bebe was in on it, too. And he could tell she was dying to spill.

"So, Bebe, you're looking great, as always," he began, stretching out next to her. He'd always gotten along with his mother's best friend, flamboyant and crazy Bebe, and he planned to trade on that goodwill now. In his experience, all it took was a little flirting to wrap her around his finger. He picked up the remote and turned the movie back on for some noise, as the sound of popping popcorn from the microwave in the kitchen offered even more cover.

"So how you doin', Cooper, sweetie?" she asked.

"Lovin' the butterflies," he teased, poking at one of her hair ornaments with his finger. "You're stylin', Beebs."

"Cooper, Cooper." She batted his hand away. "You better stop, hon, or I'm going to start taking you seriously. The men in your family..." She pressed her lips together, rolling her eyes, before announcing ominously, "You're all shameless. I swear, the Calhoun men should be hiding under a rock. True Blue Calhouns? Ha!"

Oh, really? This sounded suspiciously like what his mother had been hinting at. Narrowing his eyes and dropping his voice, he asked, "How is Mom doing, with, you know, all that's been going on with Dad?"

He figured that was a safe way to put it. If Bebe knew nothing, he could backpedal and say he was just talking about the possibility of the promotion, working too much, blah-blah-blah. But if he got lucky, she might assume he knew everything and start talking.

He got lucky.

"Oh, isn't it terrible?" she whispered, leaning closer and taking his arm. "Your poor mom! An affair with a girl like that."

"Terrible," he echoed, trying to encourage her to go on. An affair, huh? That seemed unlikely, but it was also almost a step up from blackmail and a love child. And it would certainly explain Mom's new anti-men—or at least Calhoun men—attitude.

"Him with a girl like that, and at his age. Of course," Bebe allowed, "we're not sure yet. Not till Sean finds her and hears what she has to say for herself. But what a little piece of trash. Did you see her picture?"

"Picture?"

"Your mom didn't show you?" she asked, her eyes getting even wider.

"She, uh, didn't want me to know the details," he improvised quickly.

"Ah, I gotcha. I'm sure she didn't want to worry you." Bebe gave him an exaggerated wink. "But I'm the one who took the pictures. I'm the one who saw her first, in the park, with your dad."

Woman, in the park, with his dad. Hmm... He was trying to put Bebe's pieces together with the other story. The park and a trashy woman fit Vince's version of facts, and the blurry photos, too. But Bebe was talking about a suspected affair *now*, not one from the seventies that had ended up with a mystery baby.

"You could've knocked me over with a feather when I saw him with that girl," Bebe continued. "That was when I told your mom I thought he had something going on with this chicklet, and so I went back, disguised and everything, with a camera, and sure enough, there they were again. I took their picture. In the park."

"Go figure," he murmured. What the hell was going on? Both his otherwise sane parents had sent their friends traipsing around, shadowing a strange woman and conducting surveillance, snapping pictures and eavesdropping, and then blabbing about it at the drop of a hat. Talk about weak links in the chain of conspiracy. At least Vince had thought he was Jake before he started talking. But Bebe... Cooper hadn't even tried to put the screws to her, and she was yakking her head off.

"I got those two cheaters dead to rights," she declared, clearly proud of herself. "My first undercover work."

"So you saw them sitting in the park.... Anything else?"

"Well, no. But from the way they were sitting, pretending not to look at each other, and your dad lying about where he was that day, and them both looking guilty as sin, I knew what was what," she finished indignantly.

"Uh-huh," Cooper said dubiously. So there was no real evidence of an affair, which meant that Bebe's evidence actually fit Vince's blackmail scenario much better than her theory about some ongoing love affair with a young, trashy woman. Which meant that Mom and Bebe were probably wrong, and also still in the dark about that part of it. And Cooper planned to keep it that way.

If Mom was weeping over sad movies and eating popcorn in the living room because she had some flimsy suspicion her husband was cheating, what would she do if she heard about the rest of it? Blackmail, hookers, illegitimate kids... Cooper was *so* not going to be the one to tell her.

"I knew right away," Bebe announced dramatically.

"Sounds like you ought to be the detective." He

gave his mother's friend an encouraging smile. "Sean's got nothing on you, Beebs."

"Exactly. And then, you're not going to believe this, but I saw her again! By accident. At the airport. That was just lucky, but I made it work." She shook her head, sending her butterflies wobbling. "I tailed her and everything. And, of course, I heard about..." She paused, then whispered, "Champaign."

"Champagne? Like, bubbly?"

"No, no. Champaign the city," she hissed. "I heard her say she was going to Champaign."

"Oh, downstate?"

"Yeah, that's it. Champaign-Urbana. Your mom sent Sean down there after her on Friday afternoon." She nodded sagely. "We haven't heard anything from him yet, but I just know he's going to find out exactly who she is and what she wants with your dad. You wait and see. Sean will make her talk."

So now he knew where Sean was. Two hundred miles away in Champaign. Jake on the Explorer's Journey and Sean in Champaign. Which one would really find the girl? Was there still room for a third contender? "I don't suppose I could get a look at the pictures?"

"Shh! Your mom is coming back. The pictures are over there, under one of the sofa cushions." She gestured toward the sofa. "Your mom stuck the whole envelope down in the couch when the doorbell rang. As soon as she goes back in the kitchen, you can look. You see if I didn't get some great photos."

They couldn't possibly be any worse than Vince's. "Thanks, Beebs. I'll, uh, do that."

"Everybody good?" his mother asked brightly, entering with a trayful of refreshments. She handed him a drink, off-loading another bowl of popcorn, a plate of cookies and a pile of napkins, all onto the carpet next to him. In the living room. He couldn't get over it.

Dutifully, he munched some snacks, careful not to spill anything. When his mother returned to her right mind, he didn't want her blaming him for crumbs or stains.

Squeezed between Mom and Bebe, with *An Affair to Remember* turned up to high volume, he didn't have much choice but to watch along with them. He was starting to get a headache from the goopy movie. But near the end, right around the time the main woman, Deborah somebody, got hit by a car, his mother burst into tears and ran off to the kitchen for more tissues. Good enough. Seizing his opportunity, Cooper hopped up and jammed his hand under the sofa cushions, feeling around for the envelope. *Got it.* He scooped it up and stuck it in his shirt pocket. Piece of cake.

"Hey, movie's over, so I'm gonna, um, go upstairs and see if I left my old bowling shirt up there, okay?" he announced, getting to his feet.

"What bowling shirt?" his mother asked, dabbing at her eyes with a fresh tissue.

"Just something I used to have. I, uh, need it for a party. A costume party." He was already on the stairs.

"Cooper?" she called from the bottom of the steps.

"Just take me a sec, Ma," he shouted back as he

hotfooted it to his old room. Since he knew she could hear his footfalls from downstairs, he crossed to the walk-in closet where so many of his boyhood possessions were still stored, loudly moving boxes around so it would seem as if he really were looking for an imaginary bowling shirt. Yanking the cord for the overhead light, he planted himself on a box, pulled out the envelope and began to examine the photos. Hmm...

The first one was clear and in focus, if taken from a fair distance, and it didn't take a rocket scientist to figure out it was the same scene and the same woman as in Vince's photos, murky as those were. The jeans and the shoes were a match, for one. Now that Cooper could see the scene sharply, it looked as if it was taken on the same park bench and everything. Which meant that Vince's blackmailer was the same as Bebe's "little piece of trash" and Dad had one scandal brewing, not several of them. Good to know.

Cooper flipped to the second picture, which was more of a close-up. Now he could see more of her chin, her mouth, the angle of her nose, all of which looked oddly familiar....

What? He peered down at the photo in his hand. It couldn't be, could it? Different hair color, sunglasses, but otherwise...

Cooper gulped. "It's the woman from last night," he said grimly.

Last night. In the bar on Rush Street. The redhead who'd tried to put the moves on him and said she liked guys fighting over her. She'd said her name was Tonya. What were the odds?

He stared at the picture, as if that would make the image change. But it was still her.

Cooper lifted a hand to rub his forehead, clonking his elbow on a shelf full of old board games, but he ignored the pain. Tonya. Toni. Yes, he was absolutely sure it was the same woman.

So was she blackmailing his father, claiming to be his illegitimate daughter from the seventies, as Vince had told it, or was she trying to seduce the old man, as Bebe thought? Or maybe neither?

As Cooper tried to grapple with both scenarios, trying to make sense of them, a new thought suddenly occurred to him. He already knew that his brothers were looking for her, and that they had both left town, going in different directions. Jake had taken off on the Explorer's Journey, wherever that took him, on Saturday, if the date in his dad's file was correct, and Bebe had said that Sean left for Champaign-Urbana on Friday. But Cooper had seen the woman they were looking for, live and in person, at the bar Saturday night.

Which meant that neither of his older brothers was on the right track.

"But *I* know where to find her," he said out loud.

Cooper stood up suddenly, almost toppling Yahtzee and Battleship from the shelf next to him. The bar on Rush Street. He had to go back to the bar.

THE BAR WASN'T OPEN on Sunday, so once again, his investigation had to wait. But that was okay, he told himself. He was a patient man. And he was still way ahead of his brothers, since at least he was in the right city. Yep. He was much closer to cleaning up the family mess than either of the golden boys.

The place didn't open till noon on Monday, so he had lunch elsewhere and arrived at one, trying to be casual enough so as not to cause a ruckus. He didn't want anyone calling his district or talking to his sergeant to find out what he was doing out of his area like this. So he waited for a while before sauntering over to the bar to chat with the bartender. Cooper was pretty sure it was the same one who'd been working the other night, which meant his luck was still holding. After warming the guy up, talking about how business was and how crazy the heat had been in the city, he slapped down the photo he had kept of "Tonya," a clear shot of her face. "You know her?" he asked quietly.

"Nah." The man didn't even look.

So much for the subtle approach. Cooper slid his badge onto the bar next to the picture. And lo and behold, the bartender suddenly got cooperative. "Calhoun, huh? I think I know your brother. The sergeant."

"Jake."

"Good guy."

"Uh-huh. So do you know this girl?"

"Yeah, I guess." He mumbled that he remembered her, and even volunteered that she had been a blonde till late last week, when she'd suddenly shown up a redhead.

"And?" Cooper prompted.

"She's been in here every couple of nights for the last month or so," the bartender added. "She struck me as trouble, so I been kinda keeping my eye on her. I think she must live around here. She and her husband are both nuts. Hotheads."

"Husband? You mean the short guy with the tattoos?"

"Yeah, him. Same routine every night. She'll be here, hanging out, vamping every guy with a pulse, and then the hubby comes in and yells at her to stop catting around." He shook his head. "Thursday, I think it was, he threw his wedding ring across the room. That's how I know he's her husband. He said that they were leaving Saturday morning on their honeymoon trip and if she didn't shape up, the honeymoon and the marriage were off. She crawled under somebody's table to get the ring back, and the people there didn't like it. It got pretty loud."

That sounded like an understatement.

"I guess they didn't go on the honeymoon, though, since they were back in here again Saturday night," the bartender said helpfully.

They were supposed to leave on Saturday on their honeymoon? That sounded like the Explorer's Journey, the trip Jake had taken. And Vince had heard Toni—Tonya—book tickets on that trip, too. "Yeah, I was here Saturday. I saw them," Cooper noted.

"See that guy over at the pinball machine?" The bartender leaned across the bar to point him out. "I'm pretty sure he was one of the men she was hitting on. He's a regular here. Maybe he knows more."

"Thanks."

Cooper casually ambled over to the pinball machine, where a blond guy in his twenties was racking up a pretty good score. "Yeah?" He turned his head away from the game long enough to glance at Cooper. "You need something?"

"Ever seen this girl?" he asked, sliding her picture onto the glass top of the machine.

"Maybe."

Cooper moved a little closer, flashing his badge, trying to look intimidating. "What do you know about her?"

"Not much. Hot to trot, that kind of thing." The man just kept hitting the flippers, bapping the little silver balls around. "What'd she do?"

"Don't know yet."

The pinball player slammed his hand against his machine, lighting it up for a whole lot of points. "I've got a phone number. That help?"

"Yeah. It would."

"Okay." He kept playing, and it wasn't until the last little ball disappeared in the machine that he finally fished a matchbook out of his front pocket. "She wouldn't take no for an answer. Gave me this. Told me to call her sometime." He shrugged as he handed it over. "I took it just to get rid of her."

Which was why it was still in his pocket, right? Cooper refrained from pointing that out. Someone had scrawled "Tonya" and a number inside the matchbook. Pocketing it, Cooper left the bar.

All it took was a quick call to a friend at the station to get an address that matched the phone number, and he was on his way to see Tonya aka Toni, the woman who kept popping up and making his family miserable.

The building was an old brick six-flat, kind of squatty and unimpressive, but a classic in Chicago, where these square, plain buildings with sagging porches built onto the back were common. Not high-rent, not low-rent. Just common. Tonya's number matched an apartment on the second floor, so Coop marched right up and knocked on her door, even though he wasn't exactly sure what he was going to say if she or Anger Boy were in. He figured he would just try to get the lay of the land, do some ground-work and then report back to his father once he knew more.

Here you go, Dad. I found the woman you sent Jake after. Jake came up empty, Sean came up empty and I found her. Now what?

As he considered how all of them together might clean up this family problem, he waited at the door. But there was no answer from inside. He knocked again, louder this time. "Anybody home? I got a flower delivery for Tonya. Tonya? I got a dozen roses here." Lying was getting easier the more he did it. Even he would've believed he was the floral delivery boy. But there was no response.

He was considering whether to go find the super, flash his badge and get the guy to let him in, when he gave the doorknob a jiggle. Okay, that was weird. The door was unlocked.

Cautiously, he pushed it open just an inch. The last thing he needed to do was stumble over a crime scene. On the other hand, if something was seriously wrong inside, he couldn't ignore it.

"Tonya?" he called out. "You home?"

Nobody said anything, so he carefully, slowly, eased himself inside. He was in the narrow living room, and he was alone. As he breathed a sigh of relief and looked around, the first thing he saw was, of all things, a gumball machine. He could hardly miss it. The thing was huge.

It was a complicated and bizarre gumball machine—as tall as he was, which meant it was over six foot—and it looked totally out of place in the otherwise sparsely decorated apartment. It and a lumpy sofa were the only things in the living room. A bright orange extension cord connected it to a wall socket, so it was an electric gumball machine, apparently.

On a whim, Cooper fished around in his pocket for a couple of quarters to try it out. When he'd dropped them into the slot, lights flashed on and off and a loud, zapping noise started. Sparkly confetti swirled around inside the glass dome, and then colored balls began to bounce every which way, careening off the sides.

"Whoa," he said, backing up, wishing he hadn't started the thing. It made a heck of a racket, which wasn't good when you were breaking into someone's apartment on the QT.

But it wasn't finished. As that infernal whizzing noise continued, a single gumball separated itself from the pack, shot out of a tube at the bottom, did a dipsy-doodle along a series of tracks and tunnels, before finally popping out a small door into Cooper's outstretched hand.

"Impressive," he muttered. For a gumball machine. Although it was awfully loud, and it took about five minutes to get your gumball. But definitely fifty cents' worth of entertainment.

Chewing the gum, which was pretty stale, Cooper continued to poke around the apartment. AC turned off. Dead phone. No pots or pans out, no half-full coffee cups, no cigarettes in ashtrays, nothing at all in the fridge, which was unplugged, and no evidence that anyone had been there within the last day or so.

He checked out the wastebaskets in the bedroom and the kitchen, but they were empty, and then the garbage can out on the porch, where he found a bunch of pizza boxes and a whole lot of empty beer cans. Plus three envelopes addressed to "Joey Krupke" as well as a phone bill with "Toni Jones" in the little window. He spit his gum into the can, squashing it on one of the "Joey" envelopes, and pocketed the other ones. When he ducked back inside, he perused the handy calendar tacked to the wall in the kitchen, noting intriguing markings like a loopy heart and the word *married!* on a Friday two weeks ago, and "EJ" on the previous Saturday.

From there, Cooper backtracked to the bedroom. There was still no sound of anybody coming back to the apartment, and he had located a handy exit out the back onto the porch if he should get interrupted, so he went ahead and made a more complete search. He wasn't crazy about this breaking and entering business, but the place really did look deserted.

"Hmm..." he mused, leafing through a stack of four or five brochures on top of the dresser in the bedroom. They were all for luxury hotels, including one for a spa in Wisconsin that sounded decidedly odd.

"Explorer's Journey," he read out loud. "Well, what do you know? I guess Jake ended up in Wisconsin."

Off the back of the brochure, he read, "Honeymoon exploration...explore the depth of your being and your partner's inner soul in this paradise for newly-weds. Harmony, communication and the true meaning of marital ecstasy are all at your fingertips."

This was what Jake had walked into? No-nonsense, by-the-book Jake was off exploring the depth of his being and the meaning of ecstasy with a bunch of honeymooners?

Cooper laughed out loud. He folded the brochures and stuck them in his front pocket, but continued to chuckle to himself. Dad had sent Jake off on a secret mission to find Toni, and now the boy was stuck in a newlywed nightmare, even though Toni wasn't there. It was hilarious.

Cooper was still laughing, coming up with fun mental images of exactly what Jake might be doing with his inner being, as he took a quick look under the bed and in the dresser drawers. All bare, further supporting his theory that Toni/Tonya and Joey had flown the coop.

"Okay, what's left?" Cooper pondered. "Closet."

Given the state of the rest of the place, he felt fairly sure that would be empty, too, but he might as well check it out. He swung open the door.

And out popped a woman.

She screamed, "Eee *ya!*" or something equally bi-zarre, and kicked him right in the knee, raising her hands and making slashing motions in the air. Karate?

As he tumbled to the floor, clutching his knee, all he could say was, "You're not Tonya."

3

SHE WASN'T CONTENT to merely kneecap him, but followed that up by jumping on top of him, flipping him over and wrestling him to the ground.

As they rolled around on the hardwood floor, him trying to get on top so he could gain control and her trying to flatten him, Cooper finally got a good look at his assailant. She had dark hair, almost black, and lots of it, escaping every which way from a long braid in the back. Pale ivory skin. Rounded cheeks, getting pinker by the minute. A pointy little chin.

She looked familiar. He couldn't quite place her, but from what he could see of her as they rolled around, there was something familiar...

He also noted that she was fairly tall and quite strong, that she was wearing black pants and a jacket with a white blouse, and that there was the telltale bulge of a gun in a shoulder holster under her arm. Which made his situation that much more precarious.

As he reached for her wrists, hoping to subdue her without hurting either one of them, Cooper got a hand on her breast instead. Oops. He left it there, meeting her eyes.

She inhaled sharply and spun the other direction, popping two buttons off her blouse as she smacked his arm away from her body and slammed it down on the floor next to his head. Uh-oh. Now her shirt was gaping open in the front, revealing the edges of a pretty—and rather skimpy—pink bra and the luscious curves spilling out of it. The torn blouse was probably only going to make her madder. But it sure did offer a dandy view as long as he was underneath her.

Cooper grinned. Danger, adrenaline and one hell of a sexy woman straddling him. Who could ask for anything more?

Her eyes, which were snapping with fire, were the most extraordinary shade of bluish-purple he had ever seen. She seemed to be breathing hard with the exertion of tussling with him, giving her face more color, lifting her breasts slightly, pressing them tight against the fabric of her bra and her shirt in a provocative motion that had him practically drooling.

The woman was gorgeous. He wasn't going to protest getting pinned by this lady, especially with her hips grinding into his and her open blouse offering that eye-popping scenery right in front of his eyes. All of a sudden, he was breathing hard himself.

"You're not Tonya," he said again. But she still looked familiar. Who the heck was she?

She growled, "Brilliant deduction."

"Wait a minute...." The brunette in the corner by the dart board. The one he had considered sending a drink to. He peered up at her. Sure looked like the same woman. Had everyone in the world been at that bar Saturday night? "Were you at a bar on Rush Street Saturday night?"

"No," she said flatly.

Uh-huh. He still thought it was her. "So who are you and why were you hiding in the closet? And why are you carrying a piece?" He inclined his head toward the gun in her holster. Trying to lighten the situation with a joke, he offered, "Let me guess. Paid assassin, sent by someone whose boyfriend Tonya hit on?"

"Yeah. Real funny."

"So who then?"

She seemed to consider a moment. "Don't move," she said finally. With one hand still gripping his wrist and her body balanced on his, she worked the other hand around inside her jacket, pulling out a plastic case. She flipped it open under his eyes, revealing a badge on one side and an ID card on the other. "FBI," she announced. "Agent Violet O'Leary."

"Violet O'Leary?" Her name didn't sound like an FBI agent's, and she didn't look like one, either, especially with her cheeks all flushed and that lovely display of cleavage. But he could tell from her frown she was trying hard to act severe and scary, even if it wasn't working. Still trying to defuse the situation before she decided to turn that gun on him, he joked, "Any relation to the lady with the cow? Chicago Fire?"

"I'm not from here," she countered, deadly serious.

But she released his hand, sitting back, which put her bottom squarely on his crotch. Not that he minded. He was enjoying the ride.

"Who are you and what are you doing here?" she demanded, still huffing and puffing a little, which made her breasts bob up and down in that tantalizing way. "Besides resisting arrest."

"Hey, you didn't say you were a Fed till after you jumped me. And besides..." Gingerly, he reached into his pocket, sliding out his own ID. "I'm one of the good guys."

She gave it a quick once-over, curling her lip as she scanned it. She didn't look impressed, but she did consent to get off him. Standing up, offering him a hand, she declared, "I have jurisdiction here, Officer Calhoun."

He ignored her hand. "Yeah, well, forgive me if I'm not conceding that one till I know what you're doing here." He winced as he put his weight on his knee. Damn. She'd kicked him hard. "You didn't need to kneecap me."

"Coulda shot you," she muttered. He saw her glance down at the front of her blouse, notice the gap and suddenly get all flushed with rosy color. Cute. He couldn't help smiling as she gathered the fabric together with one hand. Talk about locking the barn door after the horse had bolted.... The image of her amazing curves was imprinted on his brain.

"The, uh, buttons went that way," he said helpfully. "In case you don't want to leave evidence."

Stiffly, she muttered, "Thank you," and bent to collect the tiny white buttons that had popped off and rolled over by the wall.

"So what are you doing here?" he asked again. "Is Tonya on the Most Wanted list these days?"

"Antoinette Marie Jones," she corrected. "Now Krupke. She just got married, I guess. But she's most often known as Toni, especially Toni Jones. Tonya is one of her lesser-used aliases."

So she knew more about this than he did. So what? "Okay, so I'll call her Toni. That help?"

"Not really," she said tersely. Her demeanor was very "just the facts, ma'am" which seemed at odds with the rest of her. "If you know what's good for you, you'll leave her to the Feds. We want her. We'll get her."

"For what?"

But Violet didn't say. She reached up and plucked the hotel brochures out of his pocket and then, still carefully holding together the front of her blouse, marched stiffly toward the bedroom door. She turned back just as she reached it. "Don't touch the gumball machine," she warned. "It's evidence. I'll, uh, be back for it later."

The gumball machine? Evidence of what?

Not exactly sure what he'd wandered into, Cooper let her go. But he had to admit he was very intrigued by the feisty agent with the violet eyes and the enticing cleavage. His palm was still burning where he'd accidentally brushed her.

Even though she'd kicked him, even though the last thing he'd expected to find in Toni's apartment was a beautiful FBI agent hiding in the closet, he hoped he hadn't seen the last of Violet O'Leary. Hmm... Not particularly forthcoming with info, not willing to share sources, good on her feet... She was an interesting woman.

He shook his head. He always had had a thing for

classy, smart brunettes. And if that wasn't Violet to a T, he didn't know what was.

When he heard the front door close quietly, he knew she was gone. Cooper took his time looking around, making sure he hadn't missed anything that might be a clue to what Toni was up to or where she had run off to. Back in the living room, he took a long look at the gumball machine Violet was so interested in. What in the world could she want with it? And what crime could Antoinette Krupke have committed with a bunch of gumballs that the FBI wanted her for?

As he gazed at the machine, with all its bells and whistles, he realized he had no choice—he had to get to Antoinette, aka Toni, aka Tonya, before Violet and the FBI caught up with her. Cooper sighed. It would've been a lot more fun to flirt with Violet and see where it might lead, maybe pool their resources, even make a friendly wager on who was going to find her first, and enjoy a little more hand-to-hand and hip-to-hip combat along the way.

But he didn't have a choice. He had to find this woman before she did. If the Feds were hot to arrest ol' Toni, his friendly neighborhood blackmailer might just blab about whatever it was she had going with his dad, as a bargaining chip to try to get herself out of trouble. And bringing the FBI in on a story about his father's alleged official misconduct with hookers in the seventies and a long-lost illegitimate daughter would look very bad.

Michael Calhoun would never make First Deputy Superintendent with a whiff of that kind of scandal in the air.

Cooper plinked a finger against the gumball machine. "Sorry, Violet. You're one tempting package, but I gotta find Toni before you do. That's the whole ball game."

VIOLET HUNCHED BEHIND the smoky windows in her dark SUV, keeping a close eye on Cooper Calhoun as he walked out of the front door of the apartment building, big as life. Damn his interfering hide, anyway. She was so close to her quarry, and then some pretty boy had to waltz in and mess things up. Now she had to worry about who he was and what he knew and whether he was going to plant himself in the middle of her investigation. She'd checked for anything going on in regards to Toni at the Chicago PD, and there wasn't even a hint of trouble. So what was he working on? And for whom?

"He's hot, though," she allowed grudgingly, watching him amble along the sidewalk, limping just slightly from where she'd kicked him. Somehow the limp only made his rangy, loose-hipped walk that much sexier. Great butt, too. "Should've kicked him harder."

She shoved an errant curl behind her ear, fidgeting in her seat. She could feel hot color flush her cheeks again. All it took was the memory of her straddling him on the floor, having him dead to rights, while he smiled up at her, all cheeky and unconcerned. When her buttons inexplicably popped—and how *did* that happen, anyway?—the man had had the gall to stare down her blouse as if she were in some wet T-shirt contest.

Clutching the steering wheel, Violet told herself that she did not appreciate being treated like that sort of woman. She was a professional, damn it. And he was too hot by half, with those blue eyes sparkling with mischief, that long, lean body that was hard in all the right places when she sat on top of him, and the quirky crooked smile that took her breath away. She groaned, pushing stray tendrils off her forehead. The fact that Officer Cooper Calhoun was sending all kinds of pheromones only made the situation worse and him more dangerous.

"What does he want with Toni, anyway?" she asked out loud. She did remember seeing him at that bar on Rush Street. But at the time, she hadn't thought he was anything more than another in the endless string of men Toni liked to play with. Violet could tell he hadn't been interested in Toni. Apparently she'd figured that out before Toni had. Violet had faded into the shadows, following Toni, tailing her to this apartment, sparing no further thought for the cute guy left behind in the bar. Truly. Not one thought.

Damn his hide. She'd been tracking Toni for the better part of a year, and she wasn't about to let some flaky local cop butt in and ruin everything just when she was getting close. No matter how hunky he was.

As she watched, he jumped into a Jeep parked on the sidewalk and then drove off. She eased her own car into the street, following at a discreet distance. Flaky local cop... She suddenly wondered if he was who he said he was. The fact that he had been at that bar was kind of suspicious. Maybe he was another one of Toni's boyfriends—she always had a couple on a string—and the line he'd fed her today was just that. Maybe he was as much of a con artist as Toni.

Violet frowned at that idea. Didn't seem likely. Really, he was too good-looking to be one of Toni's men. And his pretty blue eyes were too sincere for him to be a con man.

"Oh, Violet, get a grip. He could be anyone."

It only took a second to power up her car phone and connect back with a contact at the Bureau, someone who was speedy with research, knew how to keep her mouth shut, and didn't ask any questions.

"Rosemary? Hi, it's Violet O'Leary."

"I thought you were on leave." Rosemary's voice rumbled in her ear.

"Nope. Just out of town. Following a lead on the gumball machine thing. Can you run some numbers for me?"

"Yeah, sure. What have you got?"

Cutting short the usual pleasantries, she gave Rosemary the info off his license plate. She threw in his badge number for good measure. He'd flashed it at her for about three seconds, and that was all it took for her to file it away. Violet had a very good memory for numbers and faces. That face she definitely remembered, and now she had the badge number stored, too.

Why had he been in that bar? Had he been after Toni, too? Or was he after her now because of the incident in the bar?

Violet considered the facts. Officer Cooper Calhoun. His name was too wacky to be fake. Why didn't she believe him?

"I'm just checking," she told herself while Rosemary was off looking up the data. Violet wasn't curious about him because of *him*, but because he had crashed smack-dab in the middle of her investigation. "Better safe than sorry."

By the time Rosemary got back, Violet had an address, too, since Officer Calhoun had driven his Jeep to a neat bungalow in a neighborhood a good bit south and a little west of where they'd started, and she had followed right behind.

"All three—the plate, the badge and the house— trace back to one Cooper James Calhoun, age twenty-five," Rosemary told her. "He checks out as a rookie patrolman out of the second district, which isn't far from where you are right now, if I'm reading the map correctly. DMV has him at six-two, a hundred eighty pounds, brown hair, blue eyes. And I'm looking at his driver's license picture. Humma humma. I can see why you're into this, O'Leary."

"A rookie?" She was almost disappointed. Not vice, not bunco, not a detective, just a beat cop, a mere baby who was trying to horn in on her complicated case. And if he really did work out of a station close to here, when Toni's apartment was so far north, then it was extremely unlikely he was poking around that apartment on official business.

So what the heck was an off-duty, out-of-uniform patrolman doing breaking and entering nowhere near his beat? What had led him to Antoinette

Krupke, wanted for fraud and blackmail schemes from Albany to Albuquerque?

If nothing else, verifying his ID gave Violet a renewed sense of purpose. She wasn't sitting still for any off-duty, out-of-uniform, out-of-his-jurisdiction interloper. Not in a million years.

"I think I'd better keep an eye on Officer Calhoun," she said slowly as she disconnected the phone.

She glanced at the front of the house he'd disappeared into, telling herself that her decision had nothing to do with the fact that she had gotten a feel for just about every hard muscle and toned sinew of his incredible body while they were rolling around on the floor. And it had nothing to do with the fact that his hand had connected with her breast and momentarily fried every synapse in her brain. Or that, to her eternal shame, she'd known her shirt was ripped open long before she did anything about it. She'd left it gaping, all wanton and blowsy, just to tempt him, because deep in her heart, she liked the hot, intense, riveted expression in those beautiful blue eyes.

And it certainly had nothing to do with the sad fact that when her pelvis was in perilous proximity to his, when he'd smiled that slow, sexy smile and looked for all the world as if he wanted to eat her up right there, she had wanted, for just a second, to rip off his clothes and keep on rolling around on that floor.

"Violet Louise O'Leary, you don't even know that man. You are not going to start *wanting* him after one stupid takedown on a hardwood floor," she ordered herself sternly.

Oh, yeah? *Start* wanting him? Too late for that.

Violet put the car in gear and peeled out of there, away from his house, as fast as the rented SUV would carry her. None of those silly, misguided feelings or weak-willed desires had anything to do with why she needed to keep an eye on Cooper Calhoun.

Not a single, solitary thing.

COOPER WAS FEELING PRETTY good. As he smoothed out the envelopes he had taken from Toni's garbage can, he smiled at the Chicago PD computer screen. Joey Krupke was easy. Chicago native, a couple of assault charges, one in a bar fight and one at a Cubs game, both dropped. Your usual mope who got aggressive when he was drunk, apparently. Nothing exciting there.

As for Toni... The name on the phone company envelope might be fake, but it was a start. Toni Jones, Tonya Jones, Antoinette Marie Krupke... He was running all the possibilities through the system, looking for matches. That plus the gumball machine should pull up something.

"Well, what do you know?" he mused, as a rap sheet that fit all the particulars started to fill his screen. Antoinette Marie Jones, aka Toni Jones, aka Tonya Johnson, aka Ann Marie Johnson, seemed to be a con woman with plenty of priors in several states, some involving lonely hearts scams on lovelorn losers, a few veering off into fake fortune-telling and a few in bogus investment schemes. But most of the recent ones revolved around a giant gumball machine.

He scanned the report. It seemed that she worked with a partner, usually a man but not always, and they would pretend to be gumball machine vendors, dazzling potential buyers with a really cool demonstration of one very much like the one he'd seen at the apartment. With its smoke and mirrors and pyrotechnics offering a good show, buyers were frequently moved to purchase one just like it for the lobbies of their arcades and video stores. And then, after the bucks were down, Toni and Co. would skip town with the money, leaving the poor suckers with a large empty box, just the right size for the mythical whizbang gumball machine, with a cool picture on the outside.

Kind of a fun scam as scams went, with a little more creativity and ingenuity than most. As far as he could tell, however, Antoinette Marie had no arrests in Chicago. So if she'd been selling her gumball machine in Chicagoland, she hadn't gotten caught yet.

"Hey, Coop, whatcha doin' in here this morning?" an officer named Beth asked. "I thought you were on vacation."

"I am." He left it at that, hoping she would eventually go away.

"Okay." She gave him a funny look, but moved on. Still, he decided he should finish up quickly and get out of there before anybody else got curious.

Now that he knew the gumball machine was Toni's livelihood, he also knew she'd have to go back to the apartment to get it sooner or later. So he could wait there and watch till she returned for it. But who knew how long that would take? He was up for something a little quicker.

Cooper figured he had gleaned as much as he

could from her rap sheet, but he printed it out and
took it with him, anyway. He decided to move on to
the next phase at home, where he'd have more privacy.

Driving home gave him time to ponder the issue,
and he decided that yes, this hotel thing was definitely the next step. After all, the bartender had said
that Toni and Joey, the battling newlyweds, were
planning to go on their honeymoon last Saturday.
The fact that they had dropped out of sight as of Sunday probably meant that they had done the honeymoon thing, after all.

Could they have caught up with the Explorer's
Journey? Could Jake have them under wraps even
now?

It had been nagging at Cooper ever since he'd
heard the name that he didn't know where the Explorer's Journey went, so he pulled out the computer
he rarely used, just to see what he could find. A very
quick Net search told him that the Explorer's Journey
took place at a special lakeside resort in southwestern
Wisconsin, reachable only by a special bus.

No stragglers allowed. So if Joey and his bride had
missed their bus on the appointed Saturday, they
didn't get to go on the Explorer's Journey.

"Missed your chance, kids," Cooper concluded.
And that was really too bad, for two reasons. The first
was that Toni and Joey could probably have used the
help when it came to communication and honesty
and trust and all the other things the Explorer's Journey Web site touted. And the second was that poor
Jake was apparently stuck communing with honey-

mooners and contemplating his navel when he was *so* not the right person for that, and the woman he was looking for wasn't on the trip, anyway. Poor Jake. Since Dad had been the one sending him off, all he had were those terrible blurry pictures from Vince to go on, which meant he probably didn't even know he'd missed Toni by about two hundred miles.

"Can't wait till he gets back," Cooper said with a snicker. He was trying to imagine Jake forced to lie on a mat and listen to New Age music while he interrogated his fellow zoned-out campers and looked for Toni on the side. "This is going to be a story I want to hear."

First, however, he should probably work on his own story, so that when Jake got back, he had something to tell, too.

Without the Explorer's Journey as a possible honeymoon spot, Cooper was left with the other hotels listed in those brochures he'd found in the apartment. He didn't have the ads themselves anymore, since Violet had appropriated them, but he didn't really need them. There had only been four others, and they were all in Chicago, all top-of-the-line luxury hotels on the Magnificent Mile. Quite different from the Explorer's Journey. It wasn't hard to remember the four: the Drake, the Intercontinental, the Marceau and the Ritz. Cooper had not personally stepped foot in any of them, but he knew they were fancy places, establishments that did not seem suited to Joey the Tattooed Anger Boy or Toni the Tootsie. Hey, maybe they had different ideas on the subject of their ability to fit in with the upper classes. Anyway, if they'd blown off the Explorer's Journey and they still wanted some kind of honeymoon, one of these hotels seemed like a good bet. Why else would Toni have collected those particular brochures?

He took them in alphabetical order, asking the switchboard operator at the Drake and then the Intercontinental for Joey or Antoinette Krupke, and then trying all the variations of Joseph or Joey and Antoinette or Toni or Tonya with Jones or Johnson.

"They're on their honeymoon," he offered by way of explanation, doing his best sincere-and-adorable routine. "Kind of hiding out. But we have a family emergency and I need to contact my sister right away. So I'm sorry for trying so many names, but it's important."

Whether the operators believed him or not, they came up empty on all the combinations he tried at both the Drake and the Intercontinental. But choice number three, the Hotel Marceau, was a different story.

"We have Mr. and Mrs. Joseph Jones registered in our honeymoon suite," she said pleasantly. "I'll ring."

And then, before he could say no, she did just that. He didn't even have a chance to hang up, because somebody answered on the first ring.

"Yeah?" a rather snarly voice demanded.

"Hi," he said, keeping his voice fast and chipper. "This is room service. We have complimentary champagne for you and we wondered if this was a good time to bring it up."

"No, it's not. We're on our way out." He could hear

her yell, "Joey? When d'ya think we'll be back? They got champagne for us!" before she turned back and suggested, "Maybe later tonight, okay? Like, late. After midnight. Or just leave it. You can do that, right? But leave it after midnight. I don't want the ice melting."

And then she hung up on him.

"That was definitely her," he said under his breath, replacing the phone in the cradle. "Pretty good, Coop. You found the girl, you found where she lives, and now you've got the hiding place. And what's it been, twenty-four hours?"

The other good news was that Toni and the hubby would be out, in case Cooper cared to drop by and case the joint. Which he did.

He was ahead of both brothers, ahead of Violet and hot on the trail of Toni the blackmailing gumball machine grifter. Cooper smiled as he headed off to change into his uniform and get his weapon. He might need to look official for this part of the caper.

4

STARTING AT THE TOP of Michigan Avenue, Violet first hit the Drake Hotel, but found no evidence of her target. Next up, some three blocks south and tucked behind Water Tower Place, was the Ritz-Carlton. The lobby was on the twelfth floor and she had some trouble finding it, but her hard work went for naught. No Toni.

She had left her car at Water Tower Place rather than keep moving it and paying parking every single place she visited, but she was definitely getting tired of hoofing it down the city streets on this blazing summer day. Michigan Avenue was packed with shoppers, even on a boring Tuesday afternoon, and she wished she had time to stop and get a cool drink or something. At least a bottle of water. Lugging her shoulder bag with all her lists and equipment packed inside, melting inside her standard black suit, she was really wimping out.

But finally, just when she was about to drop, she made it to number three, the Hotel Marceau, a very pretty French-inspired boutique hotel a few blocks off the main drag. Violet limped into the lobby, looking for a rest room and a drinking fountain before she hit the front desk to begin inquiries.

What she found, like a slap in the face, was that damn Cooper Calhoun, right there in the lobby of the Hotel Marceau.

"How did that bogus cop boy get here ahead of me?" Violet seethed, ducking behind a pillar where she could watch his progress. "I saw him go into the station. I was sure he would be safely riding around in his squad car, getting kitties out of trees and giving tickets to jaywalkers by now. But no. He's here, beating me to the punch."

Looking gorgeous, cool, calm and collected, Cooper was leaning on the front desk, smiling at the clerk, acting all intimate and charming, and chuckling about something. He had the whole hunky cop thing going now, with his blue uniform and his shiny badge and his weapon at his belt... Packing heat, was he?

"You planning on shooting anybody?" Violet murmured under her breath. "Or just think the ladies go for a man in uniform, especially one with a gun?"

Face it, Vi, you thought he was packing heat with or without the gun, she told herself glumly.

And she wasn't the only one. The woman behind the desk obviously shared the opinion that he was a hottie, given the way she was practically drooling. Oh, yeah. He had the hot thing covered, smug, arrogant, pretty-boy package that he was. From where Violet stood, it was patently obvious that Cooper was shamelessly coming on to the clerk to try to get her to tell him whether Toni was registered.

Violet snorted. A well-dressed man with a newspaper tapped her on the shoulder, making her spin around. "Are you all right, miss?"

"Yes, of course. Fine. I was just, uh..." How did she explain spying from behind a pillar in the lobby? She didn't. Instead, she smiled, said, "I'm fine," and ducked even farther out of sight behind a different pillar.

Had Cooper noticed her, too? No, she didn't think so. Cheerfully flirting up a storm over there, he seemed blissfully unaware that anyone was watching.

As Violet looked on from her new vantage point, getting crankier by the minute, the desk clerk slid a key his way. A key! As easy as that? He knew where Toni was and had a key to her room? Violet felt her heart plummet to her knees. If he was ahead of her, she was really in trouble.

He smiled back at the simpering clerk, blew her a kiss and backed away from the front desk. Then he took off for the brass-gated elevators at the far end of the posh lobby. Was he whistling? Was he cheeky enough to whistle when he was wooing illicit favors out of desk clerks?

Once again, Violet wanted to throttle him. And the woman behind the desk, too, just for good measure.

When the doors opened on the first car and he disappeared inside, Violet had no choice but to run over and watch the lights blink on the display above the elevator. It was the only way to figure out where he was headed. The other elevator appeared to be stuck on the seventeenth floor, while the one Cooper was in kept rising higher, not stopping, just smoothly sailing upward. Past twenty, past twenty-two, all the way to twenty-six. Tip-top.

"This better be about Toni," Violet groused, spinning back around to see if the desk clerk was still at her station. "If I get up there and walk in on him keeping an assignation with some bimbo front desk clerk..." She paused, trying to think up something bad enough. "I will just *spit*."

The other elevator was still on the seventeenth floor, not moving at all. And Cooper's was up on twenty-six. But she had to get there before he tripped over Toni, arrested her, scared her off or otherwise threw a wrench in the works. A bellman with a cartful of luggage wheeled up behind her, and three or four guests who had just checked in joined him. Violet couldn't wait for the stupid elevator to come back and then ride up with all these people, stopping at every other floor between one and twenty-six. Not when Cooper was upstairs already, possibly screwing up everything.

With an air of resignation, she hoisted her bag and headed for the stairs.

"You just better hold your horses, Cooper," she said between gritted teeth. "I'm right behind you."

UPSTAIRS ON THE twenty-sixth floor, cruising down the hallway, Cooper was enjoying himself. He'd flirted with a lot of women in his day, but he'd never considered it an official investigatory technique. Somehow he felt sure that all the other True Blue Calhouns would disapprove strongly. Dad and Jake would complain that applying charm to the situation was underhanded when straight-up honesty was the only way for a Calhoun to go, while Sean, the intuitive one, would somehow find out what he wanted to know without asking anything, just standing back and watching, reading minds, whatever it was he did in his mysterious way.

But Cooper... Well, Cooper had his own methods. And if he could get the info he needed by flirting with a pretty woman, so be it.

Suzanne, the very sweet front desk clerk, had resisted persuasion for a minute, but only a minute. And then she'd volunteered that there were three honeymoon suites occupying the whole twenty-sixth floor. She'd checked which one was the Jones', then slipped him a key with a C on it. That was easy, wasn't it?

He started whistling again as he rounded a corner and found himself in front of suite C: the Empress Eugenie Suite. Classy place. Everything on this floor was decorated in black and white with touches of gold. So he was walking on black-and-white-striped carpet and looking at glossy white walls and doors, with dainty gilded letters identifying the suites. It was elegant and pretty, and made him feel like even more of an interloper scamming his way into this place.

First he knocked. "Security," he called out, just in case they opened the door and saw him in uniform. But nobody answered. He knocked again. No reply. After that, it took just one little click of the key and he was in.

"Whoa," he said, stopping in his tracks. The place

was spectacular, with a fireplace dead ahead and a dining room and wet bar around the corner. Rickety little pieces of furniture were arranged, looking like something Napoleon had sent over from his private stock especially for the Hotel Marceau. Even the phone was ornate, a curvy black number with fancy gold trim, the kind of thing you'd feel silly holding in your hand, let alone talking into.

Cooper took a quick inventory of the living room, which had wide windows all along the far wall, with a fabulous view of Navy Pier. Pretty snazzy. The people staying here had done some serious shopping, because there were bags from Saks, Marshall Field's, Ultimo, Armani and a bunch of other retailers he didn't recognize, scattered around the suite.

"Gucci, Bloomingdale's, Pratesi," he read, looking at the bags at his feet. Sounded expensive. If Mr. and Mrs. Krupke had actually paid for all this stuff, they were moving up in the world. Somehow he doubted the loot had been acquired honestly, however.

The telephone rang, making him jump about a foot. He spun around.

"Just a freakin' phone," he chided himself, watching it ring incessantly, proving that it wasn't just for decoration.

It also proved that he wasn't quite as casual and cool about this little unauthorized spy mission as he'd thought. Not if a ringing phone freaked him out. As the sound died away, Cooper managed to convince himself to chill out and get back to his reconnaissance mission. No one was coming, Toni had told him they were going to be out till after midnight, and he could look around in peace, with plenty of time to snoop.

"No guts, no glory," he told himself, checking out the front closet and the first bathroom. If he found something interesting here in the honeymoon suite that helped him put Toni out of the blackmail biz, all to the good. If he found nothing, he was no further behind than he had been. And if he got caught, well... He would talk his way out of it.

He hadn't really had a chance to decide if there was anything useful in the suite or not when he heard what sounded suspiciously like a doorknob jiggling. Someone was messing with the main door into the suite.

Cooper slid over that way, trying the peephole, ready to step into the hall closet if necessary. But the person he saw outside the door was none other than Agent Violet O'Leary, pink in the face and gasping for breath.

"Damn it, anyway." He wrenched open the door and reeled her in. "How did you get up here? And why are you panting like that?"

"I'm not panting," she retorted, definitely panting. "I ran up twenty-six floors, so I'm slightly winded. But I'm not panting."

"Why didn't you take the elevator?"

"Because I didn't want you to... Never mind." She was wearing black pants and a black jacket again—either the same suit as yesterday, or something very similar—but a different white blouse, one with all the buttons. Too bad. He'd liked the other one. Peeling off her jacket and folding it neatly over her arm, fanning her face, she stalked right past him. "Is this it? Is this where Toni and Joey are staying?"

"You're asking me? You don't know?"

"I trailed you, okay? I saw you schmoozing the front desk clerk in that disgusting way, canoodling the information out of her. I knew she must've told you where Toni was, so I followed you."

"It wasn't disgusting and I didn't canoodle. I just asked for a key—"

"And she gave it to you. Like taking candy from a baby." Violet rolled her eyes. "I notice you didn't go to hotel security. You didn't ask for the manager. No, you sweet-talked the *girl*."

"You're just mad I got here first," he declared. "Crack FBI agent has to tie her wagon to my star just to find a suspect."

"I found the hotel independently!" she claimed.

"But you followed me up here."

"Well, yes," she admitted. "To this room, I mean. You came upstairs, so I did, too."

Damn it, anyway. He liked Violet, he really did. But he did not need to be competing with her for clues when she had the advantages of rank and expertise and knowledge of their quarry. All he had on his side was some cunning, a little charm and a strong desire to beat Agent O'Leary at this game.

As he tried to think up a way to get rid of her, she started to circle the living room, detouring suddenly—and rather haphazardly—behind the wet bar. Still breathless, she braced herself on the counter, dropping her large shoulder bag to the floor with a thud.

"I'm sorry," she murmured. "I don't feel well all of a sudden. I think I need a drink of water."

Swearing under his breath, Cooper came in behind her. He had to reach around her to get into the cupboard, which meant his arms were pretty much encircling her from behind. He could see the long French braid down her back more closely now. No wonder she was so crabby—her hair was pulled too tight. And just like the rest of her begging to be let out of that stern black suit, little wisps of hair were escaping the confines of her neatly woven braid.

"You're not going to fall down, are you?" he asked lightly, tugging at the tip of her braid. "That's all I need—you out cold, me having to haul you out of here like a sack of potatoes before our honeymooners get back." He was only half joking. She looked a bit wobbly.

As he braced her with his arms, Violet just stood there, her head tipped forward. Cooper removed the jacket from her hand, turned her around and... And wondered what she would do if he kissed her.

Why Violet was so darn cute when she was flustered and dizzy, he had no idea. But the hot color on her cheeks, the spark of awareness and anticipation in her eyes, the way her bottom lip trembled...

Man, he wanted to kiss her. Gazing down into her hazy blue-violet eyes, he was about an inch away from bending down, brushing his lips against hers, taking a taste, seeing where this amazing attraction could take them. He could tell she was overheated and a little disheveled from her mad dash up twenty-six flights of stairs, but somehow the perspiration that dotted her brow and curled the tendrils at her temples made her look even more irresistible. She swallowed. Her eyelids fluttered.

Was she shaky because he was standing so close? Or because she'd just done the StairMaster times twenty-six?

Aw, jeez. She really was shaking. "Are you feeling okay?" he asked slowly, brushing a finger against her warm, rosy cheek.

"Fine," she whispered, her eyes searching his. "Don't I look fine?"

"Oh, you look *fine*," he mumbled. That was the absolute truth. She looked better than fine. She looked edible.

It was really a shame that his True Blue Calhoun roots had to raise their ugly heads at this point, when Coop the Player would've just taken advantage of the fact that she was too frazzled to resist. But Cooper Calhoun, third son and heir to the True Blue tradition of honesty, integrity and responsibility, just couldn't do it.

Instead, he reached around her, pulled out a glass, filled it with cool water from the faucet and handed it to her, all without a word.

"Thanks." As she gulped down the water, he backed off into the living room, still carrying her jacket, feeling really disappointed in himself for turning into Mr. Nice Guy all of a sudden. "Violet, maybe you should come in here and sit down for a minute. I wouldn't want you to pass out. Honestly, I do not want to have to carry you out of here comatose. That's one even I couldn't explain to the clerk."

"I'm better now. I'll tell you, the Hotel Marceau really needs to get some AC into those stairwells. Whew." She wiped the back of her hand across her forehead, adopting a cheery, jovial tone to go with her forced smile.

He knew she was doing it on purpose, just to pretend the almost-kiss behind the wet bar had never happened. Yeah, well, he was going to catch her yet, when she couldn't hide behind hyperventilation, when they weren't both playing cat burglar in someone else's suite.

She paced around the living room, water glass in hand, and he could tell she was looking for a good place to set it down. "Maybe you should wipe the prints before you leave it," he suggested.

She nodded. All business again, she located her purse and pulled out a pair of latex gloves, which she slipped on with a vicious snap. Then she fished out a plastic bag, wrapped the glass and stuck the whole thing back in her oversize bag.

"You're stealing it?"

"I'm not going to leave a suspicious dirty glass," she argued. "They might blame the maid. That wouldn't be right."

"Oh, Violet," he muttered. "You're really something."

But she wasn't listening to him. She was snooping around more vigorously than he had, carefully extracting various wires and bits of equipment out of that huge bag, and scoping out where she wanted to leave them.

"You're planting bugs?" he asked. "Why?"

She stuck a tiny silver circle up inside the lamp, and then placed another one under the end table. "Because I want to monitor my suspect's activities, that's why. Pretty standard. But then I guess a patrolman wouldn't know about wiretaps."

So she knew he was a beat cop. Big deal. "I saw her first," Cooper argued. "In fact, she tried to pick me up. So I get first dibs in this investigation."

"You mean that night in the bar? Was that the first time she tried to pick you up?" Violet made a face at him, clearly agitated by the idea. "Please tell me that was the first time. Please tell me you and Toni didn't already, you know, *know* each other. Did you?"

Cooper ran a hand through his hair. Why in the world did she choose this to freak out about? "No, I didn't. Of course I didn't."

"That's a relief," she said darkly.

"Why?"

"Well, because..." Her chin in the air, Violet paused. "It doesn't matter why. I've been tracking her a long time, and I know her, that's all. And you wouldn't have wanted to be..." She cleared her throat. "You wouldn't want to be *intimate* with Toni Jones. She's not a nice person."

"Yeah, I kinda gathered that on my own, thanks."

"I certainly hope so." As he trailed behind, Violet moved her electronic dog-and-pony show into the bedroom. This was the first he had been in there, and it was pretty lavish, too, featuring a high four-poster bed with a major canopy over the top, lots of white linens dripping in lace, and more black-and-gold decor. He didn't see anything of use lying around, like appointment books or itineraries, but he pulled out the desk drawer and scanned inside the closet just to be sure. A man's suit, a woman's silk dress with perfume still clinging to it, a couple of pairs of shoes, pillows, an ironing board...

Violet was busy elsewhere. Pulling the chair away from the vanity, she climbed up, teetering just a little, and began to delicately thread a video camera the size of a peanut into the chandelier.

"What exactly are you looking for?" he demanded, sliding shut the closet door. "You're putting a camera over the bed? How does that help? I mean, unless what you're really doing is stockpiling tape for the Toni Does Joey Show for the Internet."

"Oh, please. This is the only overhead light fixture," she said in an acid tone. "Trust me—I am not interested in Toni's sex life."

"You interested in anyone else's sex life?" he asked, lifting an eyebrow. He plunked himself down on the edge of the bed, wrapping a hand around the gleaming, carved wood post.

"Don't flatter yourself," she grumbled.

Cooper grinned. Exactly. He hadn't had to say a word, and yet they both knew where this was headed. He was getting the definite idea that Shrinking Violet was maybe not so shrinking, after all.

"And I will point the camera at the door, okay?" she added as she adjusted the tiny lens. "But sometimes people do say incriminating things in the bedroom, you know. Sometimes they plan things out in bed."

"So you want to know what she's planning next?"

"I didn't say that."

"What are you trying to find?"

Violet gave him a hostile stare. "Maybe first you should tell me what *you're* trying to find. And why. I'd love to know why you're trailing me around, trying to get to Toni."

"Who's trailing who? I got here first," he pointed out.

"Ha!" she said with a sniff as she stripped off the latex gloves and stuffed them into her purse. "We both know who's in charge. Me!"

"We do?"

"I happen to be investigating real crimes. Federal crimes. And what are you doing?" Still perched on the chair, she set her hands on her hips. "Did you think trying to pick you up was a crime? Are you after Toni for attempted pickup with a deadly weapon?"

"Very funny." He advanced on her chair, trapping her there. "I happen to have motives of my own, which are none of your business and which involve at least one serious state crime that Toni committed here in Chicago." *On a park bench, with my father,* he added to himself. Extortion, blackmail... If he really wanted to arrest her, there was plenty to choose from. "The attempted pickup was just a coincidence and how I located her. Happy?"

"With you around, hampering my investigation?" She smiled snidely. "Not bloody likely."

Cooper jiggled her chair, enjoying seeing her totter there. "Don't make me drag you off that chair and..." But he didn't get to finish that thought. He went very still, dropping his voice to a whisper. "What was that?"

"What?"

"I heard voices. Probably out in the hall. Somebody coming?"

As they both strained to listen, they heard a scrabbling noise coming from the other room, as if someone was trying to get a key into the hole. "Damn thing isn't working!" a male voice shouted, followed by a string of more colorful curses.

"Let me try," a muffled female voice responded.

"Toni told me that they wouldn't be back till late," Cooper muttered. Fat lot of good that did them now, stuck in the bedroom, nowhere near the front door to the suite, with Toni and Joey perilously close to barging in. Thank goodness the two bozos were apparently loaded to the gills and experiencing difficulty with the key, or they already would've been in here.

He looked at Violet, still standing on the chair. Frozen to the spot, she looked down at him. "Maybe they forgot something? Maybe they will pop in and out again?"

She and Cooper sort of hovered there for a brief moment, unsure what to do.

"Do you have a warrant?" he whispered, thinking maybe they could still talk their way out of this without major damage even if they were busted.

She shook her head. "You?"

"No." No warrant to explain their presence, no convenient explanation of why they should be fooling with the chandelier in the bedroom of somebody else's suite, and no way to get back to the front door without passing the incoming guests. If they got caught, he couldn't speak for Violet or what her superiors would do, but he would be in deep, deep doo-doo.

No choice.

"Hide," he ordered.

Before she had a chance to object, Cooper hauled her and her shoulder bag off the chair. Then he tossed Violet's jacket and purse under the bed, motioning that she should go under there, too.

"No!" she whispered.

"Yes," he argued.

"The closet?"

"No. They'll open it. The bed's better."

But she wasn't moving, so he had no choice. Crouching next to the bed, he grabbed her and pushed her under first, just as loud, intoxicated voices began to spill into the suite. The voices were apparently all the convincing Violet needed. She scooted under there on the double, making room for him, too, and then angling over him long enough to make sure he didn't have any body parts or fabric sticking out under the bed skirt. She smoothed the edge of the ruffle so it covered everything down to the carpet.

"Oh." It was just a little sound, but he enjoyed it. It was the sound of Violet realizing that their bodies were in close contact, stem to stern, stuck under that bed for the duration, and that she was half on top of him at the moment. He wasn't complaining.

She stayed there, her arm on his chest, her leg thrown over his abdomen, for about a second. The air was heavy with possibilities. But then she awkwardly drew back, rearranging herself so that nothing was touching him anywhere. That was a clever trick in the close confines under the bed. Disappointing, but clever.

Cooper bent as close to her ear as he could get. "We'll just wait it out. We're fine here till they leave."

However long that might be.

"Maybe *you're* fine," Violet whispered back. She shivered.

"I can't believe you couldn't open the freakin' door!" the woman hooted, careening into the bedroom, slapping open the door with a loud thwack.

"Yeah, well, the key was stuck." He snorted, stumbling behind her, his footfalls uneven and noisy, but easy to pinpoint. "About five more minutes and I woulda been rippin' your clothes off in the hallway, baby."

He chuckled, a sound that was followed by some slurpy, moist kissing noises. "Well, we're in the room now, bad boy," she giggled. "Rrrip away, *Husband*."

"I just might, *Wife*."

Cooper saw the stricken look on Violet's face as she realized what was happening. The newlyweds were back. And they planned to make use of the marital bed. Now. The bed Cooper and Violet were hiding under. He tried not to grin, but it was pretty funny. Even Violet would admit that, right?

Nope. It was her turn to stick her lips next to *his* ear. "I do not want to listen to this," she hissed.

Cooper winked at her, but Violet just glared back. Then she closed her eyes and rolled onto her back, as far away from him as possible, folding her arms over her chest and hugging herself close, looking like a mummy in an Egyptian tomb or something. He decided it was the better part of valor to let her be. Although teasing her could've been a lot of fun.

Out there in the bedroom, there were more giggles and a squeal or two, plus some more slurps and lip smacks. Then came the long, slinky "zzzz" of a zipper and the scrape of a chair as the guy began to sing some impromptu, off-key stripper music, something about being too sexy for your clothes. It was impossible to tell which one was stripping and which one was getting the lap dance, but they were both definitely having fun out there, what with the terrible, throaty singing, the chair rocking back and forth on its legs, somebody knocking over a lamp and a whole lot of giggling going on.

Fun city. Unlike him under the bed with Violet playing King Tut. He spared her a glance. She was positively twitching with disapproval. Trying not to grin, Cooper blew in her ear. Her eyes shot open and she stared at him, either shocked or a little turned on. Why was it so much fun to torment Violet?

Outside, all around the bed, clothes were being tossed aside with carefree abandon, knocking things over right and left. Somebody let out another long moan, followed by more smoochy stuff, giggles, chuckles and noises he couldn't really figure out. Yodeling? Who made yodeling noises in the heat of passion? What the heck were they doing?

And then the bed creaked as one party or the other jumped right in with a heck of a lot of enthusiasm.

"Come on in," the man growled, bucking up and down. "Don't keep me waitin', baby."

The entire bed frame creaked every time he bounced like that, and Cooper held his breath. Next to him, Violet gulped, cringing and huddling just a little closer. Would he and Violet be sharing the splinters of a broken bed with two naked criminals at any moment? But the woman leaped in, the bed seemed to shiver, and there was no crash. Phew. It held.

Cooper relaxed. With his arm back around Violet, and her snuggled up against him, he didn't care much what the bozos up above did. Sure, it was tight quarters under here. Sure, the box springs threatened to dip into his head if the couple and their mating dance got too bouncy.

He grinned. It was still a lot more fun than any other police work he'd ever done.

5

VIOLET WAS PETRIFIED. She supposed now was probably not a good time to bring up the fact that she was slightly claustrophobic. Under most circumstances, somewhat undersize spaces were just fine. But this one, with bedsprings inches over her head, very little light, such close quarters, not enough air…

She was starting to get a little panicky. She concentrated on breathing in and out, nice and easy, not too deep or too loud, not too shallow or shaky. *Breathe, Violet. Breathe.*

It wasn't all about the fact that she was under a bed that seemed dangerously unstable, either. That heavy four-poster and thick mattress and box springs could squash her like a bug if those idiots on top got too rambunctious, and she knew that. But that was the least of her troubles, really. She had quick reflexes. She could roll if she heard a crack.

Okay, so fear of being squashed had been considered and rejected as not all that scary. *Good job, Violet.*

Number two on the list was the unfortunate realization that she was trapped down here listening to *Toni* frolicking around. Toni. The one person in the world she knew almost as well as she knew herself. She had files full of info on Toni. She'd seen and heard Toni Jones in a whole lot of different situations and cities, myriad hair colors and clothes, a variety of scams, boyfriends, partners in crime, and aliases.

But nothing this intimate. She really didn't want to know Toni this way. Yuck!

She pretended she couldn't hear. She pretended it was someone else. Heck, neither the giggles nor the voice sounded like the Toni she knew. Okay, good. It was someone else. Sure, she could convince herself of that.

But the giggling up above got louder, and so did the feminine moans. No, those weren't just moans, they were practically *whinnies*. No wonder Toni had decided to marry this one. He was sure setting her world on fire. And those grotesque noises, some long and some short, came in a rhythmic order, too. Kind of like *uh*-uh, *uh*-uh, *uhhh*, *uhhh*, *uh*-uh, *uh*-uh... All accompanied by headboard banging to the same beat.

Maybe if she treated them like Morse code, dots and dashes, she could uncover some hidden messages in those squeals and bangs. She had to do something to block out the erotic orchestra up there.

But even if she could find a way to neutralize the noise, that still left the biggest and most insurmountable problem in her current situation stuck under the blasted bed.

Cooper.

Cooper was literally breathing down her neck. The warm puffs of air coming from his very tempting mouth were wafting right over her cheek, in her ear, tickling the hair at her temple...

It was maddening.

Violet swallowed around a dry throat. If only it had been dark enough under there to block out his face. But no. Her stupid eyes had to adjust to the darkness, plus stupid Toni and her stupid husband had to like doing it with all the lights on, so even under the bed, a little light seeped in around the dust ruffle. It was plenty of light to provide Violet with a crystal clear view of how nice Cooper was to look at. And that was very nice indeed.

She was trying to control herself. Really she was. So why did he have to be so *pretty*? Was that fair? Not just irritating, arrogant, way too charming for his own good, sexy in a kind of careless, devastating way, but he had to be *gorgeous*, too? Who said that was fair?

Violet was a woman who believed in justice, in right beating out wrong, in working hard and making good choices and staying firmly on the side of the angels. This big hunk of beautiful man was sneaky, dishonest and most likely up to no good. And she wanted him, anyway. All of him.

It just wasn't fair.

At five-eight, she tended to like big men, and he was big enough. Over six feet tall. Good shoulders. She always liked good shoulders. Filling out his dark blue uniform shirt, his shoulders looked strong and powerful and just right. Amazing how he and his broad shoulders fit so neatly under this bed. Good trick. She flexed her fingers against the shoulder they were resting near, tracing the ridge of bone and sinew. Yum.

And if she let her gaze survey the rest of him, well,

she couldn't help it. What else was there to do, trapped down here, unable to talk or sing or recite the Pledge of Allegiance? There were no lists of "Things to Do" or "Leads to Follow," not under here. Nothing else to do but wallow in the reflection of his gorgeous blue eyes under those straight, golden-brown brows; that adorable nose, just a tad long, but absolutely perfect; those kissable lips, the top one a shade more narrow and the bottom one a bit more full; and that hard, clean jaw that she wanted to touch so badly it made the tips of her fingers ache. She hadn't been aware that fingertips *could* ache.

Closing her eyes, biting down harder on her lip, Violet went through a short physical checklist. She was miserable, hot, itchy, all weird and hypersensitive, and escalating out of control on the sensual side, which was not a side she was all that familiar with.

It's not my fault! she protested. What else was she supposed to think about while Toni brayed like a donkey that was getting its tail pinned and then some? Sex was in the air. The air, the ceiling, the bed, the carpet, her ears, her eyes, her mind... It was everywhere. Impossible to ignore.

And it was way too hot under the bed for this kind of sardine game. Cooper was positively radiating heat. She could feel it coming off him in waves, where her thigh pressed against his hip, where her front fit so snugly against his chest, where her arm sort of curved across him and her fingers fisted at his shoulder, bunching his uniform. She snatched her hand back.

Or maybe the extra degrees were coming from her.

Maybe it was their combined heat. Whatever it was, together they were blazing like a furnace. She could feel a trickle of sweat running down between her breasts, and she surreptitiously bent enough to pluck away the fabric and blow down the front of her blouse.

Okay, so he knew what she was doing. She could tell from the knowing look in his eye. Too bad.

Delicately, he slipped a hand up over hers, where she was tugging at her bodice, and ever so gently undid a button. One. Then two. He drew his hand away, holding it flat, putting it carefully back on his side of their cramped space.

Oh, right. Like it was a mercy mission. She could read it in that hands-off gesture. *Wouldn't want you to hyperventilate and pass out on me. Just giving you a little air.* It had nothing to do with the fact that he could now see down her blouse again, did it? Because his eyes were riveted to her cleavage.

Although she could've reached it, could've refastened it like the straight arrow she was, Violet left her blouse open, even flexed her shoulders so it gaped wider, telling herself it really was cooler that way.

This time it was Cooper who bent to blow down her shirtfront. *Oh, dear.* She thought she might die of pleasure right there, with his hot breath teasing her trembling flesh.

He undid another button. She couldn't help wiggling, shivering even though her body was light-years away from anything cold. Her gaze fixed on his long, clever fingers, those fingers that kept undoing her buttons, slowly, silently, until her blouse was open all the way down the front. He peeled it back, exposing pale skin, the creamy fabric of her bra and the taut, hard peaks of her nipples, pushing boldly against the lace. His eyes darkened. But he didn't touch her, didn't kiss her, didn't do any of the things she was hoping he might do.

Now what about the rest of her clothes? Would Cooper try to unbutton or undo anything else, purely out of mercy? Was there anything else he could get her out of?

Because she sure would've felt a lot more comfy without the rest of those bulky, bothersome clothes.

Violet, you have lost your ever-lovin' mind.

Yes, but it's scorching under here, she argued with herself. *Besides, how much trouble can we get into stuck under a bed? There's not enough space to lever ourselves into any really dangerous positions.*

It was a good argument. A big fat lie, but it sounded plausible from where she was lying.

Liar, liar, pants on fire. That much was true, anyway. Her pants were certainly on fire. Which was exactly the problem.

Cooper slid his hands inside the neckline of her shirt, making her feel all swoony and melty, making her want to get rid of her shirt entirely and feel his lips and tongue and teeth on her sizzling skin. Instead, he moved his hands to frame her face, bending nearer, close enough to meet her lips. Violet shut her eyes, almost feeling the pressure of his mouth before it reached her own.

"Oh, baby, oh, baby, oh, baby!" the woman up above screamed, flopping on the mattress. Full-throttle, she screeched, "Give it to me, bad boy! Yes...!"

Bad timing. Violet's eyes popped open just as Cooper's lips touched hers.

"You are bad, bad, *bad*...."

That *so* did not sound like Toni. Sliding away from Cooper, Violet wriggled toward the other side, edging aside the dust ruffle.

"What the hell are you doing?" he mouthed in her ear.

She batted him away with one hand while she tried to peek out from under the bed skirt, looking for clues. There was a man's shirt not too far away, but that wasn't what she needed. If she could sneak out a couple of extra inches, she might be able to snag that silk blouse over there, but it was just out of reach and she was afraid the twosome on the bed might see her if she went that far. Should she risk it?

As if on cue, a tiny bit of lingerie, a stretchy red lace camisole, came floating down from above. Violet snatched it. The item itself was minuscule, the tag practically nonexistent. But she turned it over, flipped it inside out and found what she was looking for: size 2. Size 2! Aha!

She backtracked toward Cooper, still grasping the camisole. "Size 2. That's not her," she breathed, wagging the scrap of red lingerie and then pointing upward. What a relief. It wasn't Toni! It was a stranger. Whew.

He stared at her, a puzzled expression on his face. Wriggling closer, till her face was next to his, she put her mouth against his ear. "It's a size 2. That isn't Toni."

But he still couldn't hear. The heavy breathing, the screams, the moans, the groans, the bouncing up and down, all got raunchier and more athletic all of a sudden. Violet wouldn't have believed it was possible for them to keep at it this long, and to find all those different nuances in how they panted and shrieked. What the hell were they doing?

It should have been a turnoff, but the freaky thing was, it wasn't. Not at all. She was lying against a living, breathing, hard, hot slab of man, pressed close enough to feel the outline of his revolver against her hip, and for the first time in her life, she actually had reason to ask a man if that was a pistol in his pocket or if he was just glad to see her. Or if the bulge at his hip was a pistol and the bulge nearer the center was...something else.

Hoisting herself up just a little, looking into his eyes, all she could think about was getting out of her clothes and peeling away his, feeling him skin to skin. She rubbed against him just the tiniest bit, her thighs against his. *Oh.* She could hear every kind of sex noise imaginable—and a few that were outside her imagination—and every inch of her body was dying to be touched. Violet had never felt like this in her entire life. She was shaking with suppressed desire.

And then the woman up above began to wail that frenzied whinnying "*uh-uh*" thing again, and Violet just couldn't take it. At the end of her rope, Violet forgot to keep her voice down. "What is it, the freakin' Olympics up there?" she demanded.

Cooper clamped a hand over her mouth. "Shh," he murmured in her ear.

The action stilled. "Did you hear anything?" the tart in the bed above them asked.

"Just you wanting more," her Romeo retorted.

Sounding very much as if she was in the midst of a temper tantrum, she shrieked, "Then give it to me, bad boy! You know what I want. You know what I need!"

The bed shook as he jumped up. "Just let me get the... Where did you leave the...?"

"What?" she demanded.

"You know. The handcuffs. The furry ones."

"I didn't bring them. Use your tie. Or your shirt. Rip it. Just rip it!" she screamed.

Then they heard a long rip, and the scrape of fabric being fastened around wood.

"Ooh, baby, tie me up," the woman cooed, thrashing around on the sheets. "Give it to me, bad boy!"

"I got you hog-tied and ready to brand," her husband declared, slapping something that sounded suspiciously like a bare rump. "Yee-ha!"

Violet gulped. And under the bed, fitted up against her like the yang to her yin, his hand still over her mouth, Cooper was grinning. Violet wanted to slug him. She also wanted to kiss him. Kiss him? She wanted to shove her mouth up into his and bite him. Hard. She wanted to tear his clothes off with her teeth and make love, right there, however they could manage it in that teeny, tiny space.

Listening to the sex-crazed newlyweds over their heads was pushing her past the point of no return.

She was all moist and shivery, as if she were the one who was already naked, getting tied up and rubbed down. The worst part was she knew Cooper knew it, too—that he could read it in her eyes and on her face, in the flush climbing down from where his hand covered her mouth, drifting over her neck and her breasts. She was all pink, all rosy, all *ready*.

It was humiliating. And unbelievably hot.

Whispering one last "Shh" into her ear, Cooper removed his hand from her lips, slipping it down to her breast, cupping her through the bra. She was practically vibrating with the pleasure of that one small motion.

With one finger over her lips just to remind her to stay still, he nibbled her ear and caressed her breast, pinching her nipple gently through the lace, pressing his body even closer.

His mouth dipped across hers, nipping her first, then going deeper, his tongue plunging inside more fully before sliding away again. "Oh, oh, yeah, oh, yeah..." It came from on top of the bed, not under, but it might as well have been Violet's own voice. The bed was rocking, those ridiculous people were shrieking, and Violet closed her eyes and kissed Cooper back with every bit of passion and frustration she'd been storing up for a good long time.

He had his hand on her breast, outside the bra, then inside it, palming her bare skin, tweaking her nipple, and she just about climaxed right there. Luckily, he swallowed every moan she made, and she wrapped her arms and one leg around him, kissed him back with everything she had, and hung on for dear life.

Good thing they were lying down, or she would've fallen. She had never imagined she, Violet O'Leary, would find herself underneath a hotbed of honeymooners, playing tongue twister with a rookie cop who just happened to be too sexy for anyone's good. So she forced those thoughts from her mind. She didn't think about it. She just let it happen.

She loved his mouth. She loved tasting him, gobbling him up. She couldn't get enough.

But then Bad Boy and his bride decided to move their game. As the noise over their heads ceased, Cooper pulled back. Violet tried to get his mouth back on hers, but he put up a finger, just listening.

"You start the shower," the tie-me-up girl giggled, shoving Bad Boy off the bed. With a thud, he landed on the carpet about two feet from the outside curve of Violet's bottom. Carefully, holding her breath, she inched away from the bed skirt, closer to Cooper. Above them, Bad Boy's wife squealed, "I think you're a bad, bad, dirty, dirty boy, and I need to clean you up!"

The hubby lumbered off toward the bathroom, and they could hear the sound of rushing water. "Come on in, water's fine!" he hooted.

His bride leaped off the bed, yelling, "I'm *coming!*" as she tripped daintily across to the bathroom. A door slammed. Then the giggles and moans started up again, rippling over the sound of the shower.

"This is our chance," Cooper said quickly in an urgent undertone. He rolled out from under the bed, offering a hand back to help Violet. "Come on."

"But...but—"

But nothing. He sure knew how to turn it on and off like a faucet.

Flustered, still trembling with desire, she knew that ninety percent of her brain wasn't functioning yet. But she could hardly stay under that horrid bed waiting until sense returned. At least she had the presence of mind to retrieve her bag and her jacket, both of which had gotten squished up near the head of the bed, before she crawled out as best she could. Sheesh. Her legs were wobbly. Get her excited and she suddenly became a rag doll, whereas Cooper went back to business mode without blinking. She shook her foot, pretending it had fallen asleep.

"Come on," he whispered again, grabbing her by the hand, hauling her out of the bedroom and into the living room while she tried to juggle her junk.

"Just a minute. I need to—"

He interrupted, "We haven't got time to stand around..." But then he broke off, stopping in his tracks. His voice was uneven when he said, "Oh, man."

"What?" She followed his gaze, only now realizing her blouse was completely unbuttoned, and her bra and a whole lot of skin were hanging out, right there in the bright light of day. Where was her brain?

"Button your, uh, shirt," he muttered, awkwardly taking her shoulder bag and her jacket, shepherding her toward the door again as she tried to button on the run.

"You're the one who undid it," she retorted.

"Yes, but I'm not the one who's going to be streaking down the hallway with my chest exposed."

After a quick look, he held open the door, and she scooted out. Finally. They were out of that horrible place. "Give me my jacket," she ordered, holding out her hand as they sped down the carpeted hall. "And my bag."

"You buttoned it wrong." He arched an eyebrow as he pushed the switch for the elevator. "You really want to walk around like that?"

"Oh, hell." Well, she wasn't going to redo it now. She shoved her arms into the sleeves of her jacket and closed it over her blouse. "C'mon. Let's take the stairs."

"You almost passed out after you took the stairs the last time."

Why was he so aggravating? First he'd beaten her to the room, they'd gotten trapped and he'd had his paws all over her under the bed. She'd discovered they were in the wrong room but succumbed, anyway, and they'd had make-out interruptus. And now he was arguing about their method of escape?

"But someone could spot us on the elevator." She swept a hand up and down her body. "Look at me. My hair's a mess, my clothes are all rumpled and I have no doubt I look like I just had a roll in the hay, because I did. Well, a roll under the bed, anyway. So we have to go down by the stairs. Unless you want to split up. In which case, you can take the elevator." Because, damn his hide, he looked perfectly spiffy. Not a golden-brown hair out of place. "And I will walk down the stairs."

With a sigh of resignation, Cooper did an about-face and started back down the hallway.

"So we are taking the stairs?" she asked.

He held open the door to the stairwell. "We're going to discuss our next move."

Violet nodded curtly. *Our* next move. Which meant they were moving together now. *If* she went along with this.

Inside the stairwell, she dropped her bag and sat on the top step. She had no intention of moving any farther until she was ready. After undoing the end of her braid, she fished a brush out of her purse, gave her hair a vigorous going-over and neatly rebraided it. All that pressure and pain on her scalp was a big help.

One thing was clear. The further she got away from her disgraceful behavior under the bed, the more the fog in her mind began to clear. Good. Hard, cold clarity was just what she needed. Hard, cold clarity with an undercurrent of arousal, because that was still there, too.

Cooper was hovering behind her. "You can, uh, rebutton your shirt now."

Violet counted to ten. *So* annoying. But she did go slowly as she refastened her buttons, the right way this time. Oh well. At least it gave her a chance to think about what she wanted to do next. Number one, she knew she had to get this investigation back on track. Sheesh. They weren't even in the right room! And that was totally his fault. Talk about a disaster from beginning to end.

Number two, she had to figure out a way to get Cooper off her tail while still keeping an eye on him. She had to get to Toni first, and Violet couldn't do that if he was attached to her hip or dogging her steps.

And number three, no matter what else happened, she had to keep herself from any more canoodling with him. No touching. No feeling. None.

"I think we should pool our resources," Cooper began.

"What?"

"Pool our resources. I found the hotel, I finessed the key, you've got the surveillance equipment and the connections." He shrugged as if what he was saying was just common sense.

"Finessed the key? Is that what you're calling it?" Violet tucked her shirt into her pants with a savage stabbing motion. "And a key is not a big contribution, you know. It's not like I couldn't have picked the lock if I'd needed to."

"Are you still mad about me flirting with the desk clerk?" he asked wearily. "Jeez, Vi. I got the key, didn't I?"

"Yeah, to the wrong room." Feeling defensive, she continued, "And don't call me Vi. Nobody ever calls me Vi."

"What do you mean, the wrong room?"

"I mean that wasn't Toni's room," she snapped. "That woman, the one who got hog-tied, was a size 2. I looked inside the camisole."

Hog-tied. Oh, Lord. What had they overheard? She put her hands over her ears. Would she ever be able to get those noises out of her head? *Uh*-uh, *uh*-uh... *Bang, bang, bang.*

"Look, I'm pretty sure—"

Violet held up a hand. "No, you're not sure," she said coldly, steering herself away from thoughts of Bad Boy and his shrieking bride. "I've been dealing with Toni for a long time. I've got wiretaps, photos, a whole lot of information. That is not her size and that was not her voice." A bit peeved, she added, "Which I would've noticed right from the start if you hadn't distracted me. And thank goodness it wasn't. If I'd had to hear all those sex games with Toni involved, I'd be bleaching out the inside of my ears now and for the rest of my life."

Cooper looked confused. "It makes a difference whose sex life you eavesdrop on?"

"Well, yes!" she shot back. "I mean, no. But it wasn't eavesdropping. It was an accident. And of course it makes a difference who it is. I don't want it to be someone I know. But what I can't figure out is why you thought it was her room in the first place. I just followed you. I assumed you had a good reason to think Toni was in there." Dropping her voice, Violet sniped, "My mistake to depend on you."

Cooper's golden brows lowered and he sent her a pointed glare. Apparently he didn't like being told he was undependable. "So the clerk gave me the wrong key. How was I supposed to know?"

"You could've double-checked," she groused.

"So could you."

Well...good point. She had no reason to trust Cooper or his information, and she should definitely have double-checked. Her failing. And she hated him for pointing it out. "It doesn't matter. The important thing is that we were in the wrong room and we still don't know where Toni is."

He ignored her. "We know where she isn't. Suite C. But she is in this hotel, in a honeymoon suite. Just not *that* one. I spoke to her on the phone. I know she's here somewhere. So I still say we get a room, you and I, and we—"

"Get a room? Together?" Her mouth dropped open. "Why in the world would we do that?"

"If you'd let me explain..." Now he was starting to get testy. "The desk clerk may've given me the wrong key, but I know Toni and Joey are here in a honeymoon suite. The clerk told me there are only three suites like that in this hotel, and they're all on this floor—suites A, B and C. We were in C. That wasn't it. So it has to be A or B. So we go get a room of our own, just for a day or two, however long it takes. We set up shop—a stakeout, if you will—as close as we can, and we scope out A and B. We find Toni, you wire her for sound, and bingo, we're back in business."

"Wire her for sound?" Violet echoed. "Oh, no."

"What?"

"All of my equipment is in the wrong room." She grabbed Cooper by the arms, trying to shake him. The man was solid as a rock, and she barely got him to wobble a little. "I have to get it back, Cooper. Do you know how much the camera alone is worth? I can't just leave it in their room. We don't even know who they are! What if they find the camera? Or one of the bugs?"

"Well, we can't do it now," he said calmly. "Even more reason to book a room."

Oh, brother. She hated it when he was right. Violet dropped her hands and turned away. She began to rub a spot just over her left temple, where a headache was starting to throb.

Meanwhile, he continued to detail his plan, in that same sensible, even tone that was grating on her nerves. "We'll get a room as close to this floor as we can. Then we bunk down, we use the bugs to listen so we know when the banshee twins leave, and we get back in and collect your equipment at the first available opportunity. I've still got the key, remember. Meanwhile, we also figure out where Toni and Joey really are, and plant the bugs on them instead."

Sharing a room with Cooper. Pooling resources. Her gut told her this was the worst idea in the history of the universe.

And she was still going to do it.

6

IT TOOK AWHILE to get everything set up, and that was actually a good thing as far as she was concerned. Back to the garage at Water Tower Place to retrieve her car. *Check.* Get a toothbrush, a change of clothes and some more electronics out of the trunk. *Check.* Lock everything else up tight in the trunk and set the alarms. *Check.*

Give her credit card to a new front desk clerk, stand back and keep her mouth shut as Cooper wheedled this one into giving them Suite A, which was empty. *Check.* Double-check the fact that the Joneses were supposed to be in Suite B. *Check.*

Verify that the Joneses were checked in but currently out of the room. *Check.* Verify that Bad Boy and Bride were checked in and still, er, *using* the room. *Check.*

That left Violet and Cooper with nothing to do but plug things in and wait around for something to happen. At least she could make sure her equipment was up and running before she switched it over to the right room. Violet started connecting a couple of laptops and some audio equipment on the wet bar, while Cooper mostly looked on.

"That's all you need?" he asked dubiously. "And

don't you usually have an electronics person who does that? Or at least a partner? I thought you guys traveled in pairs or teams or something."

It was not something she was prepared to discuss with him. "I'm solo on this one so I'm traveling light."

"Hmm... Solo?" He circled closer. "Why am I getting the idea this is personal for you? Is Toni some kind of burr under your saddle? What did she do, swindle your granny?"

"No. Did she swindle yours?"

"No." His grin was crooked and she had the idea her guess wasn't that far off.

Very interesting. She filed that away for later use, but made one conclusion now. Whatever he wanted with Toni, it was personal for him, too.

"Not going to give me anything more, are you, Vi?"

"Nope." Her lips were zipped. Besides, he was hardly one to talk about her odd crime-busting methodology. "How about you? Where's your partner? Riding around in the squad car without you?"

"I'm solo on this one, too."

As far as she could tell, that meant they were both flying under the radar and outside their authority. She had already decided she wasn't going to rat on him as long as he didn't rat on her. She had her reasons; she supposed he had his. She could live with that. As long as she got to Toni first and he didn't get in her way.

And now that she was in the hotel, right next door to the suite Toni might return to at any moment, it really wasn't that bad, Violet told herself. The room was huge, so it wasn't as if they had to live in each other's pockets. And she didn't even have to pay an arm and a leg for the place, since the clerk had told them it wasn't rentable because the air-conditioning didn't work very well and the sitting room furniture was being replaced after a sprinkler system accident. So Cooper had talked her into giving it to them at a rock-bottom price for their "stakeout."

"He really ought to be the con man, not Toni," Violet said under her breath. "He could sell imaginary gumball machines like nobody's business, and a little ice cream to Abominable Snowmen on the side."

"What did you say?"

"Nothing." She got back to work.

After watching her putter with video and audio and satellite hookups, Cooper mumbled something about going home, changing his clothes and picking up some supplies.

"Okay," she said lightly. "See you later then."

It took her about thirty seconds after he was gone to drop the cords, find the maid and offer her twenty bucks to let her take a quick look inside suite B. Violet quickly ascertained that the clothes and footwear in there were a size and style more appropriate to Toni. When she saw the pair of clear plastic high-heeled sandals with the imbedded glitter lying on the floor, she felt a prickle at the back of her neck. Toni had the worst taste in shoes this side of the Las Vegas strip. Always had. With the maid watching, Violet couldn't do much more than the most cursory of searches, but because of the shoes, she knew in her heart she was close to her quarry.

Back in suite A, she felt energized and stoked up. She changed into a T-shirt and a pair of shorts, ordered some room service, let her hair down, propped her back against the wall with some pillows and pulled out her handheld computer. Heaven. She was cool, she was comfortable and she was alone. It didn't get any better than that.

But Cooper would be back soon. She might as well use every minute till he returned. She planned to start with a list of what she'd accomplished so far and what she needed to do next, in a nice, straight, linear fashion.

Okay. Now she was getting somewhere. This methodical approach, by herself, with no hiding under the beds, was really refreshing.

"Hey, I'm back."

She steeled herself against reacting to his reappearance. *He doesn't faze me.* "Hi," she said cheerfully, not looking up from her little computer.

"I like the hair."

"Oh." She made the mistake of meeting his gaze when he said that. Such pretty blue eyes. So sincere. "Really?"

"Really."

She touched the dark curls where they brushed her shoulders. "I think I made my braid too tight, because it was giving me a headache, so I..." *He didn't ask about that, Vi. He gave you a compliment.* She pressed her lips together in a semblance of a smile. "Thanks."

He smiled. It was a full-out, flash-the-pearly-whites, turn-the-girls-into-mush smile, and she let herself bask in its afterglow for a short moment. It really wasn't fair, how cute he was. But then, all good con men were, weren't they? And even if Cooper didn't make his living fleecing little old ladies, he employed the same techniques to fleece front desk clerks out of keys, and unwary FBI agents out of their leads. Along with their undies. She would be well advised to remember that.

Thank goodness that moment was broken when room service arrived. Cooper was happy to munch on her food and drink her pop, and she really didn't mind his freeloading. Really. It was funny how happy it made her that he chomped on nachos with gusto and guzzled Diet Coke right along with her.

She reminded herself that the fact that they shared a taste for snacks meant nothing in the greater scheme of things. Nothing.

"I should've thought of bringing some pop from home," he told her, sitting next to her on the floor, bringing up one knee to balance the soda on. "You shouldn't be paying three bucks a can for this stuff from room service, Vi."

"Oh, expense account," she lied.

"Uh-huh." He sent her a speculative look. "That's why you used your personal credit card on the room, huh?"

"I get reimbursed later," she said quickly. "Trust me, Cooper, I wouldn't pay for this myself."

Why, Violet O'Leary, now who's the one prevaricating up the place? You tell him to trust you, when you're more of a liar than he ever was.

"Okay, well..." Best not to even think about that. She stood up, brushing off her shorts.

"I like the shorts, too." His eyes were positively twinkling. How did he do that? "You have great legs."

His gaze lazily swept up and down her body. Her calves felt tingly where his eyes brushed them, and her knees were suddenly weak. He did another circuit, and it happened all over again.

His voice got a shade huskier. "And beautiful skin. Pale. I've never seen a woman with such perfect skin, Vi."

"I told you not to call me Vi," she said automatically. Whether her skin was beautiful or not, it was decidedly pinker than normal around Cooper.

And I am not a blusher, she told herself fiercely. *I do not blush.*

Holding her head high, she marched to the other side of the room, where she had set up her laptops on the counter, ignoring the fact that his eyes stayed on her the whole way. Her voice was a little breathless when she announced, "I guess I'll check and see how Mr. and Mrs. Bad Boy are doing. Maybe they've left by now and I can retrieve my bugs."

"Bored, huh?"

"Not exactly." *Bored* wasn't the word. More like ready to jump out of her skin. Yes, that same skin he thought was so beautiful. She sighed. "I guess I just don't like waiting around. I get, uh, anxious to move on. You know, do something."

"I hear you." Idly, his hands in the pockets of his jeans, Cooper watched her fiddle with her laptop. She had it set up to get the video feed from the bedroom cam, while she was hoping to get sound from the bugs through the earphones.

So far, she was getting nothing from the camera, and not much on audio, either. Frowning, she held the earphones up to one ear, switching the receiver from one setting to the next, while she also tried to troubleshoot on the video. She didn't really need to get much, since she wasn't planning on recording anything from the Bad Boy suite, anyway, but this was a test. The equipment was expensive, and she would be really steamed if it didn't work.

"One thing, Vi." Cooper peered over her shoulders as vague images started to appear on the screen. "Why do you need the surveillance equipment? Why don't you just arrest Toni as soon as you see her? You've been shadowing her over several states, I imagine. You've got the gumball machine. Isn't that all the evidence you need?"

"Not yet," she muttered. "Right now, I'm just investigating. You know, hoping to find something I can build an airtight case out of. Mostly I want to know what her next move will be."

"Yeah, me, too. That's, uh, exactly what I want. To build a case."

He sounded really shady, and she knew very well they were both lying. But there was nothing she could do about it now.

"Oh, dear." The images on her screen came into clear, full-color focus all of a sudden. Violet gasped.

"Lordy, Lordy." Cooper came up closer behind

her. "Those two sure do know how to have a good time."

It was like watching a train wreck. A pornographic train wreck. She couldn't look, and yet she couldn't look away. What was that they were on? Some sort of salon chair, pushed out into the middle of the living room, with a blindfolded, fleshy man lying across it. Luckily, he had clothes on. Some kind of toga? But the tiny woman with him, Ms. Size Two, was wearing a pair of filmy harem pants and nothing else. She was capering on and off his lap, feeding him grapes, and she was naked from the waist up. And every time she hopped, her large, incredibly perky breasts—the kind that clearly did not come from Mother Nature—caromed up and down like big rubber balls.

Sort of stunned, putting a protective arm across her own chest, Violet murmured, "Why in the world did she inflate her breasts that big? She probably falls over every time she tries to tie her shoes."

"Somehow, I don't think shoe tying is the most important thing in the world to her," Cooper said dryly. His eyes were wide and unblinking.

Oh, for heaven's sake. *Men.* Flash a pair of gigantic breast implants in front of them and they lost all reason. "They're not even real," Violet argued, wedging herself between him and the screen, blocking his view. "They're gross."

"Well, I wouldn't say they were gross, exactly." His eyes were dancing. "Hilarious, maybe."

With a grimace, Violet switched off the video feed on the double. "Well, we know they're in their room. We don't need to watch every hideous second."

"One thing, Violet..."

She wasn't going to turn it on again, no matter what he did to her. It was illegal to spy on other people's privacy like that. She might be willing to bend here and there in pursuit of a goal, but Violet O'Leary was no Peeping Tom weirdo. "What?" she demanded.

"You put your camera in the bedroom, right? In the chandelier?"

"Yes, but I don't see what... Oh." The images had beamed from the sitting room part of the suite, with the big picture windows and the view of Navy Pier behind them. But she hadn't put a camera anywhere near there. She edged around to face Cooper. "You think they found the camera in the chandelier? They found it and moved it?"

"I was thinking maybe they brought their own camera," he mused. He reached around her to flip her screen back on, peering at it with a much more dispassionate eye than she had. All she could see was naked bodies and, well, sex. While he was cool enough to try to figure out the technology.

"I, uh..." *Focus, Violet. Think about signals and frequencies. Not body parts. Just signals.* Like the signals his body was sending hers? Was it warm in this room or was it just her? Had Cooper taken a shower during his short trip home? She leaned into him, just a fraction of an inch. Because he sure did smell good.

"What do you think?" he asked, glancing back at her. "A different camera?"

"I, uh..." Camera? What camera? Oh, yeah. "It's wireless," she said tersely, forcing herself to concentrate. "So I suppose the signals could get crossed. I'm really not sure."

"I think it has to be a different camera."

Oh, man. He was right again. She hated that. "Actually, I am sure. You're right. My camera was black-and-white. Those pictures are color. It's their camera."

Cooper's grin widened. "Mr. and Mrs. Bad Boy are taping themselves, and you tapped in."

"It doesn't matter." Her hand was shaking as she reached behind her and snapped off the screen again. She honestly couldn't look at one more minute of those bouncing silicone breasts, even reflected in his eyes, or she was going to spew.

"Well, you're right about one thing. They're still in there." Cooper situated himself in front of her, trapping her between his hard, long body and the computer. "And we're not going anywhere till they leave." He fingered a long tendril of her hair, sweeping it behind her shoulder, bending down to press his lips to the side of her neck. "What," he said softly, "do you propose we do in the meantime?"

Violet swallowed. Not this.

"Cooper," she began, searching his face. "Are you playing me?"

"Why would I do that?"

"I don't know. But you, me... We don't even know each other. I mean, I know we've been thrown together, and we've decided, temporarily, that we can, uh..." How had he put it? "Pool our resources. But still..." She licked her lips, trying to ignore the fact that his hand was trailing down her thigh. "This kind of, um, fooling around on the side, it can't be smart."

"Aw, why not?" He moved the hand that had tickled her thigh to brace himself against the counter, while he lifted the other one to play with her hair, tucking it behind her ear, tracing the wisps at her temple. Making her nuts. "We have to do something to pass the time. And this..." He closed his eyes, leaned in, kissed her sweetly, tenderly, and then drew back, leaving her wanting more. "This could be awfully fun."

Oh, that kiss was *nice*. Nicest of the nice, brief as it was. She was starting to get all melty again. Or maybe *starting* was the wrong word. Maybe she had never stopped. Violet cleared her throat. "There's more to life than, uh, fun," she said huskily, wishing his lips didn't taste so good, wishing he would kiss her again, and harder this time.

"Fun is good."

Don't do this to me. "Fun is okay, but only if it doesn't screw up anything else," she insisted. That persistent buzz of attraction and arousal just wouldn't go away.

"Hmm..." Cooper's gaze grew pensive. "And exactly what would a little fun between you and me screw up? As far as I know, we're both free agents, no ties, nobody standing between us. Right?"

"What do you mean?"

Cooper's brows arched. "Is there a Mr. O'Leary?"

"Actually, no." And there never had been. "So you're not..." She really didn't want to be curious about this, but she was. "You're not taken?"

"Nope." He grinned. "Free agent, I told you."

"You're also twenty-five and I'm twenty-eight, and..." She tried to duck under his arm, but he held her in place. "We are total opposites. We are on a case here. Or cases. And this is all a distraction. It's just wrong."

"Speak for yourself. I'm not distracted," he said flatly. "And it isn't wrong for me. Three years is nothing, Vi. You checked me out, huh? That's how you know how old I am?"

She darted around the question. "We're very different people," she told him.

"Different is good. Besides, I'm not talking about anything big." His lips curved in a half smile. He knew very well how sexy that was, didn't he? It was probably the same one he used to get keys for hotel rooms. "Just a little fun."

"You're just turned on because we've been hearing stereophonic sex ever since we got here." Violet shook her head firmly. "It isn't me. It's the spanking and the head-banging and the bondage and the harem girl and the silicone bouncing boobies."

"Wow, how did I miss that?"

"You didn't miss one bit of it, and neither did I." She crossed both arms over her chest and set her lips in a frown. "Of course you're hot and bothered. You're a man and men get that way when presented with visual or aural stimulae. But women do not."

"You trying to tell me you weren't turned on when we were under the bed, listening to the erotic Olympics?" he inquired. "I saw you, Vi. You were more into it than I was."

She had no answer for that. She was the one who'd stumbled out from under the four-poster, her knees like water, her blouse hanging open, her face flushed, her brain woozy. This was so not fair.

"I think," he said with an edge of impatience, "that you are way overthinking this. You don't have to know every detail ahead of time. Sometimes you just go for it."

"I'm not a spontaneous person."

"Today, Violet, you were a spontaneous person." He shook his head. "It might be good for you to keep going that direction, you know? Live a little. Act on what you feel. So you don't explode?"

He didn't have to turn her lack of spontaneity into a personal insult. Or a failing on her part. "Not everyone is as zesty and fun as you, Cooper," she said defensively. "And I am in no danger of exploding!"

"Says who?"

Says me! Although, of course, it was another lie. She didn't say it. But she didn't explode, either. Although she was getting darn close.

"Okay, well, it doesn't matter. We have work to do. And we don't have the time or…or the energy for that other stuff," she maintained. She pushed past him, around to the other side of the bar, and picked up her earphones. "I'm going to listen to these transmissions and try to hear something. Like snoring. They have to tire out sooner or later, don't they?"

"Not so you could notice," he said under his breath.

"Why don't you find something useful to do?" she

suggested. "Like keep an eye on the hallway so we know if Toni and Joey come home."

"Fine." He backed off, restlessly pacing around the living room of the suite, ducking into the bedroom, doing his best caged animal routine.

Cupping the earphones to her head, Violet turned away, pretending the audio was just fascinating. The good news was that her bugs were actually picking up sound now. The bad news was that it was more of the same stuff she'd heard under the bed. *Ooh, baby. You want it. Give it to me, bad boy.* With a lot of panting added on for good measure.

How much more of this could she listen to? How much longer could Mr. and Mrs. Bad Boy keep it up? And why did her ears find it sexy? It made no sense. It was gross and stupid and those people were lunatics. And yet all those noises made her want to scream. They made her want to knock Cooper onto the floor and wrestle him into submission. Or rip his shirt off, tie him to the bed with the torn fabric and have her way with him.

She couldn't get these crazy thoughts out of her head.

If everybody else in the world got to throw caution to the wind and act like idiots over sex, why couldn't she?

She had no answer to that question, except that that was not who she had ever been, and it was a little late to start acting like it now.

Oh, for heaven's sake. The bride was starting up with "uh-*uh*, uh-*uh*" again, slow at first and then faster, surging, shuddering, riding the wave.

"I'm exhausted and I'm just listening," Violet muttered. "How can Bad Boy keep going? How can she?"

Behind her, Cooper announced loudly, "Okay, I'm going to reconnoiter, see what I can find out."

Uh-uh, *uh*-uh. *Bang, bang, bang.* Violet didn't look up. She couldn't look at him right now, or bad things would happen. "Okay, well...whatever."

"Our balcony adjoins Toni's," he reported, "so I'm going to climb over. I may be able to get in that way or at least see in. I'll try the balconies, the hallways, whatever I can think of."

"Excellent. Be careful. You know, don't fall off a ledge or anything," she said weakly.

"I won't." And finally he was gone.

Violet let out a long breath, tore off the earphones and sank to the carpet. *Ooh, baby, you want it.*

Yes, yes, she did. She wanted it from Cooper. And she was running out of reasons why she couldn't have it.

COOPER STROLLED DOWN the posh hallway, trying to look nonchalant and unconcerned. He couldn't hear a peep from the lovers in suite C, but that didn't mean anything except that there was good soundproofing in this hotel. He was still absolutely certain they were in there, dreaming up newlywed games.

As he tried to find someplace he could hang out for a while that had a decent view of the doorways to both suite C and suite B, he pondered the very interesting question of Violet O'Leary. Something was going on there. Something that didn't add up.

Okay, so she was slightly whacked about this case,

definitely jittery, and she had some special stake in bringing Toni in. At least that last part wasn't weird. He knew very well it was possible to get personally involved in this kind of thing. His family was full of cops, after all, and sometimes his dad definitely got caught up in something that he couldn't help wanting to solve, wanting to put right, no matter how long it took. Jake and Sean were the same way.

So far, Cooper hadn't had any cases like that, but he knew it was certainly possible for Violet to want to bring Toni in just for the sake of the capture, for justice, for a victory, whatever. But there seemed to be something more going on than that. And she struck him as such a by-the-book investigator. So why was she going rogue agent on this one? No warrant, no partner, no team behind her. It was a conundrum.

What exactly was her agenda?

And what was with the nerves and the stress? She seemed like a powder keg, waiting for that last spark before she burst into flames. But were they flames of temper? Or lust?

"Interesting woman," he mused. Beautiful, too, which didn't hurt. But smart and feisty and innocent in some weird way that was all mixed up with the lust.

He didn't expect a federal agent to project innocence. Or smoldering desire. And yet she did.

Yep. Violet O'Leary was one puzzle he would like to solve. But meanwhile...

Was that activity coming from suite B?

It was only ten o'clock, and Toni had said they didn't expect to be back till after midnight. But from his spot near the fire door, he'd thought he heard footsteps and hushed voices.

By the time he got down there, the door to suite B was closed. He plastered his ear to it and then to the wall. Nope. Soundproof.

Still, he was pretty sure he'd heard something, and that Toni and Joey were back. Only one way to go: the balcony. He might at least be able to see something, even if he couldn't hear.

Cooper walked casually back through his suite with Violet, trying not to let her know anything was up. It was pretty low of him, but until he knew what her motives were and why exactly she wanted Toni, he didn't exactly trust her. Oh, he *wanted* her. He wanted her and a whole lot more of that creamy white skin. But he didn't trust her.

"Hey," he called out. Was there a reason she was lying facedown on the floor in the middle of the living room, her earphones in her hand, not on her head?

She kind of twitched when she heard his voice. He smiled. That was a good sign. All she said was "Mmmpf," but then her voice was muffled by the carpet.

Okay, so at least she hadn't passed out or gotten conked over the head by rival agents or something. "What are you doing down there?"

She lifted her head. "Resting," she grumbled.

All right. Resting. He couldn't help but notice that her laptop was back on, and the sex kittens were romping again. He couldn't tell exactly what they were doing from this distance, but it was bouncy.

That he could tell. And Violet had a white-knuckled grip on those earphones. Okay, so she'd freaked herself out listening and watching sex tapes, so then she'd thrown herself onto the carpet to recuperate. Sure, that made sense.

Cooper's smile widened. Violet was making herself crazy. And it was kind of fun to watch. "How are Mr. and Mrs. Bad Boy?"

"Still at it."

"Yeah, I figured."

"Anything outside?" she asked hopefully, half sitting up. "Toni? Joey? Back yet?"

"Nope," he said easily. "Not a sign of them."

Violet groaned. "If they've already blown town, I may have to kill someone. I swear if this doesn't end soon, I am going to..." She stopped. "Never mind."

Uh-huh. What was she going to do? Snap? Jump him? He could hardly wait.

With his hands jammed into his pockets, Cooper sauntered over to the balcony. He slid open the door, breathing in the fresh, summer night air. "I'm going to see if I can find anything this way. Back in a sec."

Looking miserable, Violet dropped her head back to the floor. Aw, come on. He didn't want to feel sorry for her. She was a rival. A secretive rival.

As well as a very attractive, sweet, strange rival who needed to be made love to for about six hours until she got all that tension out of her system.

Yeah, well, maybe later. Right now, he was going to play cat burglar and trip around on balconies, see what he could see, hear what he could hear, confirm whether Toni and Joey were back....

And keep whatever he found to himself.

Cooper smiled. He liked having the upper hand, especially with Violet.

7

EVERYWHERE SHE TURNED, people were making love.

Finally fed up with the audio and video streaming from the suite down the hall, convinced the honeymooners were never, ever going to sleep, Violet switched on the television. It was some trashy reality series about people hooking up on a desert island, where the show organizers plied them with liquor and tried to get them to sleep with each other in as many combinations as possible. Although she was not much of a television fan, or maybe *because* she was not much of a television fan, Violet actually started to get into it, watching avidly, scarfing up the last of the nachos and drinking the last Diet Coke, but checking the sliding door to the balcony frequently so she could switch it off if Cooper reappeared.

When that was over, she found a sleazy series about Vegas and its hookers, populated by a bunch of vapid starlets with implants.

"Oh, brother."

The weird thing was, she actually kind of liked the sitcom she hit next, about people falling into liaisons with their friends. So much skin in so little time. Maybe she was becoming numb.

But where in the heck was Cooper? Violet opened

the balcony door, poking her head out into the night air, feeling it ruffle the curls at her neck. For the first time, she was aware that the AC in their suite was fluky. Earlier it had seemed okay, but now that the heat of the day had collected up here, it was pretty hot and muggy. There was no breeze coming in off the balcony, either. The air was positively thick with humidity.

Down below, she heard traffic and sirens. Out toward Navy Pier, where she could just see the lights of the Ferris wheel if she squinted, she actually thought she heard rushing water. Probably her imagination. But no Cooper.

He must've hopped over the railing onto the next balcony and just kept going. Maybe there was an open window or door into Toni and Joey's suite, and he was looking around while they were still out. Maybe they'd come back by now and he was trapped under their bed, all alone this time.

If you had to be trapped under a bed with someone, she decided, Cooper was a pretty decent choice to get stuck with. Okay, he was an awesome choice to be stuck with.

Damn him, anyway.

She padded to the far end of her balcony, leaning over as far as she could to try to see into the next suite. *Don't look down*, she warned herself. Between the balconies was nothing but the street, twenty-six floors away.

Next door, the drapes were pulled, she noted. Tilting and stretching like that did not afford her the greatest angle in the world, and there was no way to know if Toni and Joey were in there or not. If she knew Toni, probably not. That girl liked nightlife. With the convenient excuse of a honeymoon, Toni would probably be up all night drinking and dancing.

Besides, Cooper was supposed to be watching the entrances. If they were back, he should've been on it, and then immediately reporting in to tell her so.

So where was he?

Violet briefly considered leaping over the railing and jumping the gap to the next balcony, too, but it was a long way down there, and she wasn't really equipped for aerial work. She could've done it, she told herself, but a safety harness and the right clothes would've been nice. Nope. Better to let Cooper take on the daredevil and high-wire part of the partnership.

As she turned back to their suite, she decided she should be glad he wasn't back yet. At least this way she could ponder her new sensory overload in private.

Back inside, she picked up the earphones, almost disappointed to hear snoring coming from the bedroom of suite C. Wow. They'd finally had enough of each other. Go figure.

In a strange way, that made her even more apprehensive. Like, okay, they'd had their turn. *When is mine?*

It was so weird, because that was just not like her. She happened to be a person who never considered sex all that important. Most of the time she didn't think about it at all. So was this new, bizarre state of constant arousal because of Boobsie and her Bad Boy?

Or because of Cooper?

Unfortunately, Violet knew the answer to that one. She always had been a teacher's pet, the first one in any classroom to have her hand in the air.

Me, me, call on me!

Any D student would know this one, however. It was that obvious. There weren't even multiple choices. "The answer," she said out loud, letting her words waft across the empty room, "is, B, Cooper. It started with Cooper. Damn him, anyway."

Her switches had started to flip the minute she'd jumped out of the closet on top of him, the minute they'd tussled on the floor. She hadn't exactly known what was happening yet, but that was definitely when this crazy out-of-control attraction had begun.

Damn him, anyway. Why did he have to go bringing sex into her equation? She'd been so happy as an undersexed, obsessively committed federal agent, thinking about nothing but busting bad guys, dogged in her pursuit of Toni the gumball machine swindler. And now...

Now finding Toni was a distant second priority. Maybe third. Because first was figuring out how to seduce Cooper while making him think it was his idea. And second was doing it again really quickly once she'd done it the first time.

Unfortunately, she was going to need Cooper to come back before she could even think about how one accomplished that sort of feat. Maybe he had ditched her completely. Maybe he had spotted Toni and Joey and followed them off to parts unknown. Maybe setting up this stakeout had all been a ruse to keep her occupied while he arrested Toni and dragged her off to the Cook County Jail.

"Oh, hell, Violet, maybe, maybe, maybe. Maybe a lot of things," she snarled to herself. "You just can't borrow that kind of trouble."

Although borrowing trouble was actually something she was pretty good at. Worrying about something, planning for all the contingencies, usually meant the bad things never happened at all. "Worry insurance," her mother called it. Violet thought it was a fine system.

How odd that this was one time she wanted the thing she was worried about—making love with Cooper—to come true, not go away. For once, she wanted to cash in her worry insurance and just go for it.

She stretched herself out on the floor and contemplated the ceiling, mulling over her options. "Sometimes you just have to trust people. What has Cooper ever done to you? You checked him out, he's really a cop, and for some reason, he wants to catch up with Toni. Well, so do you. He didn't abandon you under that bed or give you up back at the apartment. He didn't yell when you got snippy with him. And he didn't push when you withheld information. Give him a break, will you?"

And give yourself one, too.

Maybe Cooper was right. Maybe there was nothing wrong with a little fun of the sexual variety to pass the time. The women on TV sure practiced that theory.

"So here's the deal," she said aloud, setting it out for herself. "If we try it and it doesn't go well..."

If it didn't go well, if the combustion between the two of them was just a mirage, then she would know that and stop obsessing over it. And that would be good, wouldn't it?

On the other hand, if it did go well, if they burned together with the white-hot intensity she suspected, well, then... Violet swallowed. Then she just might not ever be the same.

"Vi, are you still on the floor?"

She jumped when he slid open the door to the balcony, walking through as big as life. One moment, not there and the balcony was empty. The next, presto change-o, there he was.

She gulped. Could he read her mind? Was her emotional instability written all over her face?

To cover, she launched into a rush of words. "Oh, thank goodness! You were gone so long I was starting to worry you fell off." When she laughed, it sounded hokey and artificial even to her own ears. "I, uh, figured if you went overboard the cops would be here by now, but still..."

"Nope. All in one piece."

And a darn fine piece it was. She looked a little closer. What the heck? Why was he toting groceries? "Chips? Beer? How did you get that?"

"Went shopping."

"Yes, but..." She shook her head. "Does the balcony lead to a minimart or what?"

"No, the balcony leads to a fire escape, which has a window that opens into the maids' storage room. You know, the place with all the towels and the tiny soaps. The window was open. I think the maids sit out on the fire escape and smoke. Lots of cigarette butts out there." He smiled, offering her a bottle of beer out of the cardboard carton. "Want one? They're still cool, if not cold."

She waved it away. "Wait a minute. You walked out of the maids' room, but...then what?"

"I walked out of the maids' room, down through the lobby and went shopping," he said, as if it were the most sensible thing in the world.

She still didn't get it. "But if you were coming from the lobby, why did you come back here via the balcony? Carrying potato chips and beer? You could've just walked in the front door."

"Well, yeah." At least he had the grace to look a little sheepish. "It was more fun that way."

"Cooper, you went balcony hopping when you didn't need to, carrying a bag of potato chips and a carton of beer?" The more she said it, the more ridiculous it sounded. She felt like smacking him for being so reckless. "Balcony hopping, on the twenty-sixth floor, toting packages? Are you insane?"

"Oh, come on. It wasn't that hard. You just scoot over the railing. There's only about four inches between balconies. And then, of course, a slightly wider gap between the last balcony and the fire escape." He brushed past her, pulling the silver ice bucket off the counter and starting to shovel cubes into it from the freezer behind the wet bar.

Well, he just had all the answers, didn't he? Violet didn't know what to think anymore. This was supposed to be her investigation, with him along for the ride. He was supposed to be the lightweight, the rookie, and she was supposed to be the expert. But he was turning into Superman all of a sudden, leaping small balconies in a single bound, leaving her behind like some stodgy, stick-in-the-mud version of Lois Lane. Balcony hopping. *Really*.

Violet stared at Cooper with a kind of awe and maybe hunger. No, she definitely did not know what to think.

"Listen," he explained after a moment, "I do have info. The first time I went out there—when I left here, I mean—I went right into Toni and Joey's suite. They didn't lock their door, either. I guess people don't expect anybody to walk in off the balcony twenty-six floors up."

"Oh." Toni and Joey's suite. Violet had almost forgotten about the real reason they were both here. "So you got into their suite. Find anything interesting?" she asked in her best innocent voice.

"Not much. Definitely her place, though." He frowned as he began to shove beer bottles into the ice bucket. "The person who set me onto her had a picture of her wearing these awful shoes, and I actually saw the same shoes in her room."

"Oh, man, the 'ho' shoes? I know exactly what you mean. I saw—" Violet broke off, remembering again that she hadn't told him she had cased Toni's place while he was gone. Quickly, she made up a new story. "I saw those before. In Toledo or someplace. I don't remember. Plastic, sparkly, really high heels, with an ankle strap?"

"Yeah, those are the ones," he said thoughtfully, giving her a very strange look.

"Hideous shoes."

"Uh-huh."

She bit her lip, wishing Cooper didn't look so suspicious. She'd mucked up the story about the shoes, and there was really no reason to keep it a secret from him that she had been in the suite. She just didn't want him to know she had waited till he was gone, and done her search behind his back. It was awkward. "And that was all you saw? The shoes?"

"Yeah, pretty much. Some clothes, not size 2." He kept his eyes on her. "Otherwise, they travel light. And I didn't see any handy-dandy notes around, like addresses or phone numbers or schedules or anything. But like I said, I definitely think that's her suite."

"Well, that was good work, Cooper," Violet allowed, offering him a smile. "Excellent work."

He nodded, keeping his own counsel as he pulled a dripping bottle out of the bucket, twisted the top off and took a swig.

"But..." Violet hesitated. One part of his story was bothering her. "You still haven't said why you came back in here through the balcony," she reminded him. "I mean, except for the fact that it was more fun. You left here, you scouted out their suite, you kept on going around the outside of the building, you came in through the storage room and you went down to the lobby. Then you went shopping. And then you came back up from the lobby with your groceries and went back out on the balcony." She shook her head. "Excuse me, but that's really silly when you could've just waltzed in the front door."

"You're really a stickler for the details, aren't you?" he asked with an amused glimmer in his eye.

Politely, she noted, "I like things to be linear."

"Well, you're right about the sequence. But I did have a reason, as it happens." He stretched out his legs as he hitched himself against the counter, tipping back his beer every once in a while. "Y'see, when I came back upstairs and got off the elevator, it dinged again about two minutes behind me. The other elevator was stopping on this floor, too. The doors opened and Toni and Joey got off—"

"They did? You saw them?"

"Yep. And as soon as I spotted them, I ducked back inside the storage room. They didn't see me." He shrugged. "So they toddled off to their room, while I sneaked around outside, by way of the balcony, and listened at their windows."

Wow. This was getting good. "You did?"

"Yeah. You can hear a lot more from the windows than you can from the hallway, by the way." Setting his bottle on the counter, he ripped open the bag of chips and started munching.

"So?" Getting anxious, Violet leaned over the counter. She reached past him and gingerly extracted a single chip. "And what did you hear?"

"Nothing much. They went right to bed." Looking quite unconcerned, he continued to chomp, punctuating it with a swallow of beer.

But Violet wasn't happy. "That's it? You play Superman, broad-jumping balconies while hauling groceries, and all you get out of it is the fact that they went to bed?"

"Sorry. That's what I heard. At least it wasn't—"

"Okay, okay." She held up both hands to shut him up. They both knew what it wasn't. Like maybe what had been going on over in Sex Suite Central all night. Thank goodness. "You're sure they turned in, tucked in, dozed off?"

"As sure as I can be. I listened for a while," he assured her.

"Damn it. I wish I could hear them." Violet took a look at all the useless electrical equipment sitting there. She threw her uneaten potato chip down on top of the audio receiver. Toni and Joey could've been plotting to knock over the mint tomorrow, and all she could get on her wiretaps was panting, moaning or snoring from the suite beyond.

"You didn't miss anything," he said quickly. "They came in, the lights went on in the bedroom, they were muttering at each other, maybe some kind of minor dispute, and then everything in the suite went dark and completely quiet. Nothing exciting. No plotting. No clues."

"Okay." What was up with Cooper? Why was he trying so hard to convince her?

"What about the lovebirds?" he asked, hooking a thumb at the laptop.

"The video cut out a while ago—I think they shut off their camera, and mine never did start working. All I'm getting on audio now is snoring, so I guess they finally called it a night, too." Her tone dropped into a huskier range, something she hadn't intended, when she added, "That just leaves us, I guess."

Cooper was on that in a flash, leaning across the counter, taking her hand. As he looked down at her, his blue eyes took on a smoky hue. "Leaves us for what? What are you trying to say, Violet?"

"I didn't mean anything by it," she began, glancing away, but she knew he knew she did.

"Are you ready to turn in, too?" he asked softly. He rubbed his thumb into her palm in soft circles, and she trembled. "Or something else?"

Oh, Lord. Why was she so easy to turn on and off? It was as if she had a switch concealed somewhere and Cooper knew exactly where to find it. "Turning in, um, might be good," she managed to answer. Her voice had acquired a funny shake, a strange ripple, that didn't sound at all like her.

"You're looking a little overheated again, Violet," he murmured. He pressed his freezing-cold beer bottle to the side of her neck, and the shock of it made her gasp. "Better?"

"In a, uh, way," she stammered, her wide, uncertain gaze searching his face, as he slid the wet, chilled bottle to her temple and then back down to her collarbone.

"Uh..." She opened her mouth, but only one small, inarticulate sound came out. Icy condensation from the outside of the glass slithered down inside the neckline of her T-shirt, and her whole body tensed, on sensual alert. As her head tipped back, as her eyes pressed shut, as the beads of chilled water dripped down inside her clothes, she felt as if she were steaming from the inside out, hotter and more aware of her skin than she had ever been in her life. The mix of heated flesh and tiny drops of cold water was... unbelievable.

As she shivered with the sensation, he skirted around the bar, bridging the distance between them, and then she found herself leaning into him, hooking an arm around him, waiting to see what came next.

"Violet?" His voice was gruff as he bent down to brush his lips against the cool spots the bottle had left, right behind her ear, on her jaw, on her neck.

He slipped a hand under the bottom of her T-shirt, and the chill of his hand, still cold from holding the bottle, was another small, exquisite shock. She flinched as his fingers skidded higher, grazing her ribs. All she could do was whimper and try to keep standing.

"You still look too hot to me." He licked her ear, biting down gently on her lobe, still sliding his hands around, dancing along the waist of her shorts, back to her belly button, up almost to her breast. "Maybe we should take off your clothes, let you breathe."

"No," she demurred, swallowing despite a dry throat. She wasn't quite ready to go there yet.

"Hmm..." He reached over, took a handful of ice and chilled water, and splashed it on her front. "Cooler?"

All she could do was gasp. More cold, cold water splashed over her as he tossed another handful and then another. "Cooper!" she cried. "I'm soaked."

"That was the general idea."

She stared down at her plain white T-shirt, now plastered to her body, outlining her bra, displaying her taut nipples in sharp relief. She felt a rush of pleasure course through her. Cold and wet and...on fire. "I might as well be naked."

He smiled. "I know."

"You are a wicked, wicked man," she breathed as he bent his head to lick and suck her skin through the T-shirt. A moan escaped her as he bit down on one peaked nipple. She splayed her hands in his soft, honey-colored hair, clasping him against her.

But he rose, covering her mouth with his, holding her tight, pressing her up into him, exploring her with his hot, delicious kiss, delving deeper, pulling away, deeper yet... Making her want him even more.

Her shirt was rubbing his, transferring moisture and cold, and he stepped back, cursing under his breath. His eyes were intent on hers, and she realized that joking, flirtatious Cooper had left the building. This was a man with a purpose. And that purpose appeared to be ravishing her. Her eyes widened.

He peeled off his shirt in one easy motion, revealing an absolutely gorgeous torso, all gleaming skin and hard muscle. Mouthwatering. His hands went to the top button on his jeans.

She held her breath.

The rivet snapped, the zipper zipped and his jeans slipped all the way down to the ground. He kicked them off, standing there in nothing but a pair of tighty whities. She could see the long, hard ridge under the front flap, and she tried to remember to keep breathing, keep taking in air, so she didn't just faint on the spot.

She moved closer, reaching for him, dying to touch all of him, but he backed away. Instead, he motioned that she should do the same. Strip? Just like that?

"Maybe I could..."

"Take it off, Violet," he said, his heated gaze never leaving her.

It was time to make up her mind. Pull away, say no, huddle on the carpet with her gun and her badge and her wiretaps? Or hang on, say yes and tumble into ecstasy with Cooper?

"Yes," she whispered. "Yes." And she pulled the wet T-shirt off over her head and threw it away.

"And the bra," he whispered roughly.

She unclasped it behind her, letting it fall away from her body. His gaze devoured her bare breasts. She thought she might hyperventilate.

"And your shorts."

"Oh." Trying not to stumble, not to look clumsy, she hooked a thumb under the waistband of her shorts, turned away slightly, eased them down an inch over her hips, and then another inch. She'd never stripped for a man before, and this outfit didn't make it easy. Three pieces so far. Too easily disposed of. There was no way to make it last or anything. And underneath...

Steeling herself, she slipped off her shorts and tossed them off to the side, revealing the tiny thong she wore.

"Oh, Violet," he said in a husky groan, "you continue to surprise me."

"Surprising?" Standing before him, with his eyes raking her, she felt a new, sharp pang of hunger deep in the pit of her stomach. Before it had been a fuzzy, dizzy tingle; now it was a hard, hot coil of desire.

But... But she knew her hair was a tumble of crazy curls in this humidity, that her skin was pale and plain in the still room. As for the thong... It covered absolutely nothing. Those minuscule panties had seemed like a good idea when she'd bought the package of six for her trip. So small, so easy to pack. And oddly comfortable. But now, with one little ribbon of fabric and her entire bottom exposed, the thong seemed like a terrible idea. With him looking at her that way, with her bones turning to water, she didn't know what to feel or say.

"Um, surprising?" she asked awkwardly. "Is that good?"

"Oh, yeah."

She didn't have to say anything more. Cooper swept her up in his arms and carried her into the bedroom.

Their decor was different from suite C, thank goodness. They were more country French, with a brass bed and pale lavender embroidered linens. And this bed was lower to the ground. Nobody hiding under there.

Cooper held her about a foot over the bed and then dropped her. She fell back into the pillows with a whoosh. He was smiling as he rolled in with her, immediately catching her, tangling their arms and legs together.

He had his hands everywhere, starting more fires

than she knew what to do with. She was breathless, dazed, leaping from one sensation to the next. If she'd had plans to do a more thorough exploration of his body, she didn't have a chance. Cooper was just too quick for her.

His mouth on her breast was incredible, so much better than through the T-shirt. Just when she was getting into the rhythm of that, lifting herself up and into his mouth, hanging on to him by the shoulders, he moved on, his hands curving around her bottom, pulling her on top to rub up and down his lean, rigid length. New places, new nerve endings started to throb.

She didn't know when she lost her panties. But they were gone when he started kissing and licking her belly, suddenly, unexpectedly dipping lower, practically sending her leaping off the bed with the intensity of the pleasure. "You're going to have to scrape me off the ceiling when this is over," she said shakily.

But then she couldn't say anything. His tongue... Oh, my. Oh, my.

Violet clutched at the sheets with both hands, unable to stop herself from hurtling up and over the edge, so fast and so hard she truly couldn't breathe for a second, as his clever tongue darted in and swirled over her. Gasping for air, she lay back, enjoying the ebb and flow of sensations, shattering hard, as Cooper held her, stroking her, until it felt as if every last drop of pleasure had been wrung from her limp, sated flesh.

But then, with a quick kiss, Cooper slid over the side of the bed and away for just a second.

"Where—" was all she got out before he was back. He kissed her quickly and fiercely, tickling her, making her giggle and squirm and want to do it all over again.

"When do I get to turn the tables?" she murmured, trying to grab on to something as he pinned both her hands over her head in one of his and lay flat across her body. She wasn't really complaining. His way had been amazing so far. And she felt so satisfied, so relieved, so energized, even as she curved a leg around his hip, trying to pull him in for more.

"Hold on to the headboard," he said in a sneaky, smug sort of tone.

"What are you up to?"

"Just do it."

"If I do, will you give me what I want?" she teased, hooking her leg all the way around him, rubbing him suggestively.

"I already did." He kissed her lightly, on the lips and then the tip of her nose, pulling her wrists up to the headboard. "Hold on to one of the posts. C'mon. Do it."

"What, hearing Bad Boy rip up his shirt made you want to try it, too?" She sighed. She was in no position to argue, not with Cooper on top of her and her hands trapped like that. So she did as she was told and clasped two of the brass spindles over her head. "Just don't rip up anything of mine."

"Good girl." Kneeling over her, Cooper made a

swift motion, she heard a loud clink and she felt cold metal circle her wrists.

"What?" She tried to raise up off the bed, but she couldn't get very far, not with her wrists manacled to the bed. She yanked, but the cuffs held fast, already biting into her skin. "I—I'm not so sure about this," she told him. "I'm a little uncomfortable with the kinky stuff. And I'd rather be able to touch you. So unlock it, okay?"

But Cooper was scooting off the bed, backing away, heading into the living room.

"Cooper?" she shouted. She pulled herself as far up as she could get. Having both wrists in cuffs and the chain between linked around one of the spindles in the brass headboard didn't give her much leeway. "Cooper?"

Pulling on his uniform pants, zipping himself up, he offered, "Sorry, sweetie."

"What do you mean, sorry?"

He smiled. Damn his hide. Why was he smiling? And why was he putting his uniform on? "Well, the good news is that I'm not into the kinky stuff, either, so you're safe on that score."

"Then why am I lying here handcuffed to the bed?" she growled.

After shrugging into his shirt, he stepped back and just looked at her. She hated every one of her body parts for pulsing like that as his hot gaze flickered up and down her body. "I have to tell you, that was really nice, Violet." His eyes were warmer, softer now. "Man, you don't know how much I would love to stick around."

"Stick around? What do you mean?" she asked in fresh alarm.

"You see, I lied, Violet."

Her head fell back into the pillows and the handcuffs clanked to the bottom of their respective spindles. He'd lied? Yeah, well, there was a surprise. "About what?" she asked grimly.

"I did hear something when I was on the balcony." Completely dressed now, his gun at his belt and everything, he stood well out of her reach. And then he had the gall to look apologetic as he hefted his duffel bag, ready to depart. "When I was eavesdropping outside their balcony door, Toni and Joey were packing up. They were congratulating themselves about their great plan to get a free honeymoon by sneaking away in the middle of the night and skipping out on the bill before the hotel figures out they left some other Joe Jones's credit card."

"You heard all that?" Violet closed her eyes. She was a chump and she deserved it. Her mind had been on sex, not on business, and she hadn't been watching Cooper closely enough. Not in the right way, anyway. "And you didn't tell me?"

"Well, I would've, but, you see, I need to get to her first. And this is my shot." He checked the watch he'd just strapped on. "Their escape is planned for, oh, twenty minutes from now. Once they leave the hotel, it'll give me enough to hold them on credit card fraud and theft. So right now I'm going to follow them. And I just can't risk having you horn in on my collar."

"It's not your collar," she snapped.

"It is now." He leaned over far enough to kiss her,

and she did her damnedest to bite him or knee him or get a good kick in. But it was no good.

"Don't worry, Vi," he offered as a parting shot. The damn man was positively grinning as he turned in the doorway. "Once I get rid of Toni, I'll come back. Shouldn't take more than an hour or two. And then we can pick up where we left off." He shook his head. "I gotta tell you. This pose looks amazing on you. I can't believe I'm crazy enough to walk away when you look—" he exhaled a shaky breath "—like *that*."

"Do you really think you can pick up where you left off? Get a grip, Cooper!" she shouted, rattling the cuffs against the brass bed. "Watch your back. I am so on your tail! You may be ahead now, but I will catch up!"

But then he was gone.

Violet considered screaming like a banshee, but she already knew from Bad Boy and Boobsie's escapades that no one would hear. These rooms were very well soundproofed from the hall.

Besides, how embarrassing would be if someone did come in to rescue her and she had to admit she was an FBI agent stripped and manacled to the bed?

She was going to have to kill him. That was all there was to it.

She was going to have to kill him. With her bare hands.

8

BEHIND THE WHEEL of his Jeep, Cooper whistled aimlessly as he watched Toni and Joey try to wedge the last of their bags into their little red sports car. Just think, he could've been upstairs with Violet, warm and cozy in the brass bed, playing games all night long.

Cooper ran a hand over his face, rubbing his eyes. Not even dawn, and he was on surveillance for a couple of mopes, instead of in bed with Violet where he should've been. It was idiocy. "Good time to start picking business over pleasure," he told himself. And Violet was pure pleasure.

Violet. It had been worth it to watch her melt like butter on a hot griddle. Worth it? He closed his eyes for just a second so he could replay a little of that action. All that creamy, pale skin, so soft, so luscious. Oh, yeah. Getting a few licks in with Violet was definitely worth what he was suffering now. And would suffer later, when she caught up.

His smile returned. It was fun, in a crazy sort of way, to be a step ahead, to know she was coming after him with fire in her eye. He couldn't wait till she got here.

Of course, if he was lucky, he'd have the whole

Toni matter cleaned up and disposed of before Violet arrived. That would probably tick her off even more, to be Violet-Come-Lately, to have her quarry already out of sight and out of mind. Angry Violet was Fun Violet, if last night was any indication.

Of course, he realized with a frown, there was a possibility Violet could just move on, too, once Toni was out of the picture. Places to go, new grifters to bust.

"Maybe," he mused aloud. "Or maybe not. Maybe she'd like to stick around awhile." He grinned. "Maybe she'd like to pay me back for the handcuffs." Now that idea had promise.

His attention was pulled back to the parking garage when Joey threw one of the shopping bags out of the car, scattering boxes and parcels onto the cement with a loud clatter. Then Toni, whose hair was now blond again, pitched a fit, yelling at Joey and waving her arms around. He was holding his own, though, gesticulating and swearing right back. Ah, yes, the happy couple.

It seemed they had acquired too many items to fit in the small vehicle.

"You should've thought about that," Cooper said out loud in the privacy of his own car. "Especially when conducting credit card fraud, never buy more than you can carry."

Finally, after several more minutes of drama, they were all packed into the car somehow, and swung out toward the gate. Since it was so early, the garage was mostly deserted, and Cooper kept his distance as his targets pulled up at the gate. The attendant wasn't there—another perk of leaving before dawn—and they sailed through without paying.

"They are really catching all the breaks, aren't they?" Cooper said with a certain sarcastic edge. "Yeah, well, that's gonna be over soon."

He trailed them easily down Lake Shore Drive, staying far enough behind, camouflaging himself behind cabs and buses and whatever else was handy, till they turned onto the expressway, where there was enough traffic to blend in. He could tell they weren't expecting anyone to follow just by the way Joey kept driving like a maniac with his head turned toward Toni, and they kept yammering at each other. Finally, they took an exit, winding around for a bit before stopping at an auto repair yard in a pretty nasty neighborhood. No clue what this was all about.

As Cooper kept watching, patient and inconspicuous, Joey got into a white panel truck, while Toni stayed in the sports car. Cooper spent a moment deciding which one he was going to follow, but it turned out it didn't matter. Toni and her red car stayed demurely behind the panel truck, all the way back north to their apartment.

"Jeez, if I'd known they were coming here, I could've saved myself a lot of hassle following them across town. What are they doing back here, anyway? The place looked cleaned out."

All except for the gumball machine. Oh, yeah. The gumball machine.

As he kept an eye on them from his Jeep, the newlyweds pulled their panel truck into an alley behind the apartment building. They both went upstairs, and

Cooper parked his car about a block away, preferring to get a closer look on foot.

He chose a good vantage point on the porch next door, and saw them come back down several minutes later, struggling to navigate Toni's back stairs with that big, clumsy gumball machine.

First they argued for about ten minutes because Toni thought that something Joey did had made her break a nail, and she told him in no uncertain terms that the manicure was expensive and he owed her a new one. Then she got fussy about the speed with which they were descending the stairs.

"Joey, you're going too fast," she whined. She was wearing tight jeans with the famous clear plastic high-heeled hooker shoes, and she was having trouble not falling right off her shoes. "We gotta be careful. You drop this thing and I'll kill ya, I swear."

"I ain't dropping it. You just watch your end." He slowed up and they made it down finally, resting the machine on the ground for a break.

Toni was already flitting back and forth between the truck and the gumball machine. "All right then. We need to prop that back door open, because if it slams while we're loading my machine, and you drop it, I will never forgive you."

"Stop with the dropping the thing, will ya? You're just asking for trouble," he said angrily. "I swear, you keep putting ideas into my head and I *will* drop it, just because you said it so many times. Power of digestion, y'know?"

"It isn't digestion, you moron. Suggestion. Suggestion." She gave him a good poke with one of her long scarlet fingernails. "Why'd I ever hook up with you, Joey? You better keep your mouth shut if we try to sell this baby, because no one's gonna believe a word you say. I do the talking, you understand?"

"You need to stop telling me what to do," he retorted, bristling. "Now pick up your end and let's load this thing on the truck and get outta here."

"Open the door first, you moron!"

Cooper was trying to decide when would be the best time to jump in and cause the least fuss. Taking out his badge, he stepped out from the cover of the next-door porch, approaching cautiously. "Antoinette Marie Krupke?" he asked. "Could I speak with you, please?"

Immediately, she looked ready to fly. He could see her shoot a glance at her precious gumball machine, at her husband, at Cooper, at the gun at Cooper's belt, and then do the whole circuit again. Apparently she came to the conclusion she had nowhere to go, because her shoulders sagged and she asked in a sulky tone, "What do you want?"

"I'd like to speak with you and your husband. But not out here." He inclined a thumb at the stairs. "Why don't we go back to your apartment and have a chat?"

"Why should we do that?" She chewed her lip, gnawing through the remains of last night's lipstick, regaining some of her bravado. "We were just loading up our property, which we have the perfect right to do. There's no reason for you to interfere. C'mon, Joey." She signaled him to get around on the other side. "He can't stop us."

"Well, actually I can." Cooper stood resolute, between Joey and the machine. "There's the little matter of credit card fraud, theft of services from the Hotel Marceau, and the fact that you are in possession of this gumball machine, which is itself evidence of fraud in about seven states."

"You don't have any new charges on that," she blustered. "I was arrested and it didn't stick, and I've been clean. It's no crime for me to own my own gumball machine."

"But it is a crime to use that other Joseph Jones's credit card," he returned. "I've got plenty to arrest you on and detain you for a while, and in general, make your life very uncomfortable."

Toni fidgeted. Next to her, Joey started to get antsy and red in the face, as if he wanted to pop Cooper one, but she held him off. "I get the idea you're offering something else, where that arrest and detain stuff wouldn't have to happen. Am I right?"

"You just may be. Which is why we need to talk."

"Upstairs?" she inquired, walking a bit closer, putting a swing into her hips. "Are you sure someplace else might not be better? And maybe just us two? You know, leave Joey here?"

"Wait a minute." Joey bristled again. "I ain't—"

"Joey, chill." She held up a hand.

Cooper got the idea, if Joey didn't. She wanted to get Cooper out of the way so Joey could secure the all-important gumball machine while they were gone. "No, we'll include Joey. And we'll do it upstairs. I don't think you want your neighbors seeing you chatting with a cop in the alley any more than I want to be seen doing it."

She crossed her arms and fixed him with a stubborn stare. "I am not leaving my gumball machine down here while we go upstairs."

He should've figured that one. "All right then. The three of us will carry the thing upstairs, and then have our chat."

She nodded. "You better be damn careful with it."

Cooper just bent to pick up his end, not dignifying that remark with a response. From there, Toni pretty much directed traffic as the two men hoisted the stupid toy, and she hovered around nervously while they maneuvered it cautiously all the way up the stairs to the apartment.

"Set it down there," she ordered, insisting it go back in the living room. "Careful. Gently. Gently, I said!"

"It's not made of eggs," Joey grumbled.

"It's not made of cement, either."

"All right, all right," Cooper interrupted, already tired of their squabbling. He'd only been around them for a few minutes, and it was already getting old. "The gumball machine is fine where it is. Why don't we sit down and discuss this thing like rational adults?"

Toni waited until he pulled a chair in from the kitchen, and then she perched herself on the lumpy sofa. Joey remained standing, looking like an undersize bodyguard as he hovered beside her, doing his best to project a menacing attitude. Cooper didn't feel menaced, but he gave Joey points for trying.

"Okay, then." Toni met his gaze squarely. "What are we discussing here? All I know is you been making threats, and I don't like it. So why don't you come across with whatever it is you want from me, and make it easy on everybody."

Joey nodded vigorously. "Yeah, make it easy on everybody."

Cooper decided he was ready to be done with these two jokers. "Here's the deal," he said curtly. "I don't really care what you're doing. Just get out of town. In fact, get out of the state. You can take your gumball machine off to greener pastures and richer suckers. I really don't care. As long as you never come back to the state of Illinois and never go near my father again."

"Who the hell is your father?" Joey growled. "What has he got to do with anything?"

Toni peered at Cooper, not saying anything, chewing on her lip, speculating.

"Wait a minute. You look familiar," Joey declared, tipping his head to the side and squinting. "Ain't I see you before?"

"Yeah." Cooper clenched his jaw. "Rush Street. Saturday night. You threatened to beat me up."

"Aw, man," Toni groaned. She slapped herself in the forehead. "I remember the bar, but... You're a freakin' Calhoun. I should've noticed. How many kids does that man have? Your brother was nosing around our honeymoon trip, messed up the whole thing. That freakin' thing was expensive, too! There he was in line with some woman, pretending to be on the Explorer's Journey. He's a dead ringer for your old man. Minute I saw him, I knew what was up."

"Oh, you saw Jake."

"Saw him, recognized him, ditched the whole trip because of him." She shook her head. "And now you show up. A girl tries to earn a little extra cash and the whole freakin' family comes down on her head! What is it with you people?"

"Calhoun?" Joey demanded, shifting his feet, looking restless. "But we saw him at that bar Saturday night. He was trying to hit on you."

"No, she was trying to hit on *me*," Cooper corrected.

Toni rolled her eyes skyward. "It was just a little misunderstanding."

"The bar has nothing to do with this. That was a coincidence. This is about my father." He was trying to get them back on track here, even though he was really starting to think all of this was a bad idea.

Still, he knew it was the way his father wanted it to be. Avoiding a scandal was number one on Deputy Superintendent Calhoun's priority list. It was just that more crimes had been committed now, and Cooper was feeling less and less sure this was the right way to go.

"I just want to come to an agreement," he said, trying again. "Like one where you and Joey vanish and don't bother my family anymore, and I forget all the illegal activity I've seen you engage in. I should arrest you right now. Letting you walk is all kinds of wrong. But I'm willing to offer you this chance just to make life easier for my father."

"So I asked your dad for some cash. It wouldn't have killed him to stake me," Toni scoffed.

"Which one is Calhoun?" Joey ducked down closer to hear her answer. "Is he the president of the car company?"

"Joey, that was in Detroit. Sheesh. Calhoun is the police guy, up for a promotion." She pressed her lips into a sour grimace. "I should've known better than to go after a big-shot cop this time. Politicians work better."

Just to make things perfectly clear, Cooper asked caustically, "So I take it you're not my long-lost sister?"

"Hell, no."

"Or doing the nasty with my old man?"

"Who said that?" Toni demanded. She leaped off the couch, advancing on Cooper and teetering on those ridiculous shoes. "I never went near him. Sure, I tried to get some money out of him. But I never slept with him. Never. I don't sleep with marks."

Joey's face was taking on new hues of red. "What is he talking about? Who is he talking about?"

Cooper stood up, too, and backed toward the kitchen. If Toni and her long red fingernails got any closer, he wanted to be able to defend himself.

But Joey was stuck on one concept. "Toni, he said you hit the sheets with his old man!" he thundered. "Is that the con? Sex now, pay later or I'll drop a dime?"

"No!" she shouted. "I said I was his freakin' daughter, okay? Classic love child con on somebody who had reason to pay up to keep it out of the papers."

"Because if you fooled around with that guy..." Joey let out a screech and started to twitch with rage, waving his small fists in the air, making the tattoos on his biceps vibrate. "If you did—"

It was at that exact moment that the wooden front door to Toni's apartment splintered into a million pieces. As Cooper whirled around at the sound of the crash, Violet burst in, with a pair of handcuffs still dangling from one wrist.

Toni's eyes went wide. "You kicked my door down?" she demanded. "You kicked my freakin' door down?"

"Whoa," Cooper murmured. That was impressive.

"FBI," Violet announced, extending her weapon in front of here. "Nobody move."

Cooper couldn't help smiling. Violet was impressive in full-on Fed mode, that was for sure. She was wearing the standard black pants, but a plain white T-shirt, not the starchy blouse or the suit jacket. It didn't matter. She still looked fierce. He still couldn't quite believe she'd kicked that big honking door in. Too bad the others weren't really paying attention to her. Busy with their domestic dispute, they were missing a heck of a show.

"I don't care who kicked the door in," Joey roared. Clearly, this was too much commotion for his tiny brain to handle. He bent down and pulled a compact .22 out of his boot. Waving the little gun in the air, he demanded, "*Who* did you sleep with, Toni? I want to know now."

"I can sleep with whoever the hell I want to, whether it's this Calhoun or his father," Toni yelled. "Get over it and put that thing away."

"*This* Calhoun? So you slept with this one?" The wail that came out of Joey stopped everybody in their tracks. He spun around and headed straight for Cooper as the nearest target, catching everyone by surprise. At least he wasn't pointing the gun; it was hanging limp in his hand, forgotten. Before Cooper had a chance to react, Joey dipped his head like a miniature bull and rammed it into Cooper, slamming him into the living room wall.

It was as if the scene around him had started to run in slo-mo. Cooper saw Joey coming at him. He reached out to hold him off, to push the gun away, but his back hit the wall, his head snapped and he actually saw stars.

He could hear, he could see, but he couldn't move for the next few seconds. He heard a sharp crack and the sound of shattering glass, and then another crack, as gumballs started rolling everywhere.

"Oh, no!" Toni's scream was full of anguish. "You shot my gumball machine!"

The sound of Violet's voice, commanding, "Everybody freeze!" threaded through the chaos, but nobody froze. Dropping his gun, Joey bolted past her through the remnants of the front door and Toni made a beeline in the opposite direction. Meanwhile Cooper lay there like a beached whale, gasping for breath.

"Toni. Go after Toni," he gasped, but it came out more like a few wheezes than words. Jeez, was he shot? Nah, he wasn't. So what was wrong with him? Why couldn't he move?

But Violet ignored both fleeing suspects, speeding to Cooper's side instead.

"Toni. Out the back," he managed to yelp. He was starting to be able to draw a small amount of air now.

"Yeah, I saw her." Her face was tight as she knelt to examine him. She unbuttoned the front of his shirt and peeled it aside, holding the fabric away from his body, delicately checking for wounds. The handcuffs attached to her right wrist were cold where they brushed his torso. "I ought to shoot you myself. You do realize that, don't you?"

"I'm not shot," he wheezed. "Just...I don't know."

She started poking around, a lot less gently this time. "It's kind of red, but there are no holes in you. I think he knocked the wind out of you. Maybe bruised a rib or two with his hard little head. But nope, you're not shot." She took a deep breath. "Too bad."

Now that air and sense were returning, Cooper started to feel a tad embarrassed. "Aw, Violet, don't hold a grudge. Maybe you should just leave me alone." He batted her hands away. It was incredibly humiliating to get knocked to the ground and taken out of commission by a runt like Joey. Cooper preferred to do his recovering without Violet there, thank you very much.

"You know, what I really should do is leave you here by yourself to explain this to all your pals on the force," she said as she stood up. "Hear the sirens? Somebody obviously reported the gunfire. So unless you want to share what you're doing here and why you're shooting to kill gumball machines, I suggest we make tracks."

Struggling to his feet, Cooper muttered, "I didn't shoot the damn gumball machine." He patted his weapon, still in the holster at his belt.

"Well, it wasn't me," Violet protested.

"Joey pulled that girly gun, the .22, out of his boot. It's on the floor somewhere. Must've been him."

Violet bit her lip, and he could tell she was trying not to laugh. "I don't think he did it on purpose. Poor Joey. He shot Toni's meal ticket and she'll never forgive him."

"Better he shoot the gumball machine than he shoot me. I mean, as long as he was going to spray bullets around. Could've been a lot worse." Shuddering, Cooper pushed away from the wall. "All right, Violet. Let's get out of here."

Was that a smirk on her face? "Be careful," she said sweetly, offering an arm to help prop him up. "Wouldn't want you falling down on any gumballs."

THE CLOSER THEY GOT to Cooper's house, the angrier Violet got. She knew he was injured and she shouldn't be so snippy. But she also knew he wasn't injured that badly, and after the stunt he'd pulled, he deserved far more than mere snippiness.

Part of it was still the handcuff thing, although really, the less said about that, the better. Because if she called him on that, then they would both remember that she'd been naked when she was handcuffed, and why she'd been naked, and what exactly had happened before the handcuffs came out.

In other words, they would both be simultaneously creating mental pictures of a whole lot of stuff she didn't want to think about.

So she took that righteous indignation and let it spill over into the other part of her mental distress, the part that kept replaying the sound of gunshots and the sight of Cooper sliding down the wall, his face looking stunned. It was awful. And upsetting.

"Look," he ventured from the passenger seat, "I don't like the idea of leaving my Jeep."

"You just don't like me driving, me in charge," she shot back. "You're injured. You're not driving. and your Jeep is fine where you left it parked. We got your stuff out of it. It's fine."

"Listen, Violet, I know you're mad at me. But—"

"But nothing. You played me and you got what you wanted."

"Well, technically, you got what you wanted, too." He gave her a crooked smile. "Actually, if we're being specific, you got more than I did."

Holding herself rigid, Violet stared straight out the windshield, refusing to acknowledge that. Oh, she knew exactly what he was referring to. And if they were being precise, technically, she had attained a certain level of satisfaction that, uh, he did not. "Your choice, not mine," she said under her breath.

How utterly aggravating that when it came to matters of sexual self-control, Cooper Calhoun was about ten steps ahead of her. She was all wild and wanton and coming apart at the seams, while he held it together easily enough to walk away before he even...

The whole issue was beyond embarrassing. She hoped her face wasn't as pink and hot as it felt.

"I'm not sorry about that, Vi, I'm really not," he insisted. "I loved every minute of you and me and that bed. So you can be mad all you want, but that doesn't change the fact that we had a great time."

"A great time?" With her hands on the wheel, the handcuffs clinked every time she made a turn, mocking her. She pursed her lips, still refusing to look at him. "You don't happen to have a key for these ridiculous handcuffs, do you?"

"I left it."

That got her to glance his way. "What do you mean, you left it?"

"On the desk in the bedroom. I thought you'd need it."

"But you didn't tell me." She let out a small groan of frustration. "I worked the whole brass rod out of the headboard to get myself off that stupid bed."

Cooper's grin was even more annoying than anything else he'd done. "I would've liked to see that."

"I'll bet you would," she said coldly. She swerved the car into his driveway, screeching to a stop. "You seem to enjoy mocking me."

"I wasn't—" he began, but she cut him off.

She had him dead to rights. "We were supposed to be pooling our resources, sharing our information, and you lied," she told him, keeping her chin up and her emotions in check. "You staged that whole seduction thing just to distract me and humiliate me so you could get to Toni first."

"That is not true." Shifting in the seat, he gazed at

her with those pseudosincere blue eyes. "It was exactly what I said it would be, which was a way to pass the time till we could get on with the hunt for Toni."

"Pass the time." He made it sound so simple. And meaningless. And casual.

"We were both bored out of our minds. We were both stressed out of our minds." Cooper raked an impatient hand through his hair, sending a shiver through her body as she remembered having her own hands in his sleek, soft hair, pressing his head as he...

She clenched her jaw, hard. Maybe she should recite the Declaration of Independence till those thoughts went away.

"It was also something we both wanted," he added with a certain intensity. "And it was fabulous and I'm not going to apologize for that. Tell me you didn't want it. Tell me you didn't need it. Tell me you didn't enjoy it."

"Well, I sure didn't enjoy the betrayal." Without another word, Violet jumped out of the car.

9

HIS HOUSE WAS FURNISHED as plainly as she expected. Not that she had really thought about it, but he struck her as the kind of guy who ate and slept at home and nothing much else, and the decor in the bungalow bore that out. Hey, he had more furniture than Toni, she'd give him that.

Violet had a few minutes to look around as he brought in his duffel bag, plus the items she'd toted from the hotel. She'd already told him in no uncertain terms to get everything out of her car, that she was not storing his beer or his potato chips or anything else he'd left behind in the suite. Too bad she hadn't noticed the key to the handcuffs when she'd done a high-speed sweep of the hotel room and tossed everything in her SUV.

"How did I miss that key?" she muttered, glancing down at her ridiculous bracelet.

Behind her, Cooper ducked in long enough to say that he was taking a quick shower. As she heard the sound of rushing water coming from somewhere in the back of the house, she focused on the small display of family photos framed and set out on top of the entertainment center. She certainly wasn't going to think about naked Cooper all wet and yummy in the shower. No way.

And it was interesting to see some faces from the Calhoun family, anyway, to put this whole deal of him protecting his father in better perspective.

He hadn't said a whole lot about his family, but the first photo she noticed was a head shot of a middle-aged man who must be his dad, looking stern and proud in a police uniform. Deputy Superintendent Michael Calhoun was printed at the bottom of the photo. Next to that stood a wedding picture with a sweet, innocent-looking bride in a peasant dress, holding a bouquet of daisies. Must be his mother.

There was also one of three boys in Cub Scout uniforms, and another with the boys grown to men, now in dark blue Chicago police uniforms. Whoa. Violet picked it up to examine more closely. Blue eyes, wide shoulders, more good looks than you could throw at a stick at. That was a whole lot of man power to pack into one little picture.

So not only was every male member of the family a cop, but they were all gorgeous. And Cooper was the youngest. Interesting.

Before she knew it, he was back, still damp from his shower, his hair wet and his skin sparkling, looking totally scrumptious in what appeared to be a pair of cotton pajama pants and a half-unbuttoned dress shirt.

Looking somewhat serious, he inquired, "So where do we go from here?"

Violet didn't answer. Did he mean "we" as in "the two people who got naked together"? Or "we" as in "us two law enforcement types who have legal matters to resolve"?

"What do we do about Toni?" he clarified finally. "We know she's out there. And neither one of us got the collar."

"Cooper, I heard you, back at the apartment," Violet told him, reluctantly meeting his eyes. It had been a genuine relief to overhear him making Toni that offer. And while it didn't mitigate her anger over other things, it was still nice to know that they both wanted Toni out of town more than behind bars. "I heard you offer to let her walk if she would just leave town. So I know you never planned to arrest her."

He shrugged. "I would've told you, but... It's a family thing. Nothing I can really talk about."

"Well, actually, I heard that part, too." She shuffled her feet. "About your dad, and Toni trying to extort money from him. I'm sorry."

"Not your fault. That's our Toni," he said briskly. "Always looking out for the main chance."

"Well, uh, if we look on the bright side," Violet murmured, wondering why the heck he didn't dry off and put on some more clothes and stop torturing her. "She won't be pulling her gumball machine scam again anytime soon."

"Yeah, but that probably means she'll increase her efforts on the blackmail and extortion fronts to keep herself occupied and flush." As casually as if he were in the men's locker room, he began to unbutton his shirt. "It's so stupid. Anyone who knows my father knows he would never have been involved with a prostitute or had a kid out of wedlock. It just isn't in him."

He was undressing? In front of her? Why? Should she tell him to stop? "I—I believe you. About your father, I mean," she stammered.

"Thanks." His smile was warm. Too warm.

Her eyes widened as he dropped the shirt into his duffel bag. Uh-oh. She could feel herself starting to weaken again. Not just because he had stripped to the waist and she got a clear look at those pecs and abs again for the first time since they'd been in bed with her. *Don't drool*, she ordered herself, staring at the floor. So what if he had accidentally left his clean shirt in the duffel bag and now felt the need to change in front of her? No biggie.

No, it wasn't just the strip show. It was because she was beginning to understand his motives, and why he wanted to get to Toni and neutralize her. Because the twit was blackmailing his beloved father, claiming to be his illegitimate daughter, and threatening the whole family. The scenario was similar to cons Violet knew Toni and her entire family of con artists had pulled in the past, so she wasn't that surprised. And of course Cooper had stepped in to protect his dad. Who wouldn't?

Although that didn't justify the unlawful restraint and aggravated assault against a federal officer....

Oh, hell. Time to admit she hadn't been a federal officer when she was being restrained. She'd been a woman in the heat of passion who got exactly what she'd wanted. Passion.

"Cooper, I—" she began, but she didn't really get

to finish the thought, let alone the sentence. Now he was starting to take off his pants! What the heck was going on here? "What do you think you're doing?" she demanded.

His brows lowered. "What?"

"Cooper, you can't take off your pants. I mean, not in front of me!" she protested.

"Why not?"

"Well, it just isn't..." What could she say? That it wasn't nice? Polite? Fair? "Smart," she finished lamely.

"It's nothing you haven't already seen," he noted, giving her that crooked smile as he ducked behind the sofa long enough to doff his pajama pants and shrug into a clean pair of jeans he'd pulled out of his duffel bag.

Staring a hole in the floor, Violet retorted, "Yes, but I don't necessarily need to see it again."

"Okay, okay. My jeans were in here, so I thought I could just change here rather than waste time taking everything into the bedroom." He snapped the rivet at the top of his jeans. "Better now?"

Not really. Because the whole idea that he was casual enough to just pop out of his clothes like that and not even care that she was standing here had her all mixed up again. She hated being mixed up. Plus she now knew that he was wearing a pair of faded jeans with absolutely nothing underneath. "Half-naked is only slightly better than—"

Her words were cut off by a loud pounding on the front door.

"Cooper, open up!" The voice was male, deep, irate and quite loud.

She could see the look on Cooper's face, and she knew that the person at the door was someone he was in no hurry to greet.

"Cooper, this is your father," the newcomer said ominously, giving the door another good whack. "Open up or I'll shoot it open, you hear me?"

Cooper went to the door.

"Hi, Dad," he said with a studied lack of concern as he swung it open. He just sort of lounged there, hooking a hand over the top of the door. "What's up?"

His father—looking very much like he did in his official Chicago PD photo, except without the uniform and the hat—barged in around him, forcing Cooper to get out of the way. A smaller, older man trailed slowly behind, blinking behind thick glasses. After letting them both in, Cooper sent Violet a rueful glance.

Not exactly sure what part she was going to play in this, she backed up to the sofa and sat down, sticking her arm under her thigh to hide the handcuffs. But the senior Mr. Calhoun didn't seem to notice or acknowledge her presence. His focus was all on his son. And he didn't look happy.

"I just got a call from that girl!" he blared. "Toni. Toni the blackmailer. Now she's upped her price to two hundred thou and she wants it brought to the park by noon or she'll go to the papers with the cockamamie love child crap. She says she's doubled her price because you shot her gumball machine. Gumball machine? What the hell is that supposed to mean?''

"I didn't shoot it. I didn't even have my weapon drawn.''

"I don't really care whether you shot it or not. I care that you have made a complete hash out of everything!''

"Dad, I can explain—''

"What are you doing, sticking your nose in my business?'' his father demanded. "How did you even know about it? Did Jake tell you? Because I told him to keep it quiet. I trusted him.''

"No, actually, Jake didn't say a word. But Vince did,'' Cooper allowed. He inclined a thumb at the older man. who was standing there looking utterly confused. "It wasn't his fault, though. He thought I was Jake at the time.''

"What?''

"Well, I can tell now he's not Jake,'' the man identified as Vince offered. "I mean, I'd know he wasn't Jake because Jake wouldn't be hanging out half-naked with a strange girl at six in the morning.'' He peered at Violet from behind those glasses. "Hello, miss.''

She put her free hand to her brow, hiding her eyes. While she did not appreciate being called a "strange girl," she was desperately attempting to figure out exactly what they were saying. Processing the clues quickly, she decided that one of the brothers in the picture must be Jake, and their father had trusted him to investigate Toni, not Cooper. In fact, Deputy Superintendent Calhoun seemed surprised and upset that his youngest son knew anything about it. So Cooper was a volunteer in all this.

"Cooper, if I had wanted you to come roaring in like a bull in a china shop, I would've asked you," his father snapped. "But you knew something was up and decided to go poking around on your own, huh?"

"Jake and Sean were on the wrong trail," Cooper said quietly. "I decided someone should be on the right one."

"What does Sean have to do with this?"

"You sent Jake. Mom sent Sean."

"She *knows?*" Michael Calhoun bellowed. "Your mother knows about Toni and the blackmail?"

"Actually, I don't think so. She thought..." Cooper paused briefly. "She thought you were having an affair, Dad."

"Oh, Lord, this is a nightmare." Michael Calhoun began to pace back and forth, swearing under his breath. "Well, boyo, you wanted to play the hero. You wanted to find Toni. And you found her all right, didn't you? Of all the harebrained—"

He didn't get to finish that insult. Someone else was beating on the door, drowning him out. Violet was actually starting to enjoy this. It was kind of fun seeing Cooper on the hot seat. Who would it be now?

This time a female voice, just as irate, just as loud, shouted, "Cooper Calhoun, open this door and let me in!"

Cooper and his father exchanged glances. They were both looking decidedly green around the gills. "Mom," Cooper announced.

"Oh, my," Violet said out loud. She couldn't wait to see his mother.

Mrs. Calhoun didn't wait to be invited, just pushed right through the door. She was a pretty woman, not tall but quivering with an indignation that gave her a certain amount of presence. She had light brown hair streaked with blond, stylishly cut. And the same penetrating blue eyes as her son.

Violet sank lower into the sofa, really not wanting to meet Cooper's mother under these circumstances.

"Your door wasn't locked." Cooper's mother glared at everyone in the room, and even Violet flinched under that merciless gaze. "And you were not going to keep me out."

"Hi, everybody." A newcomer, a smaller woman with platinum-blond hair done up in shellacked curls, came in right behind her.

"Hi, Beebs," Cooper offered. "Blond now, huh?"

"You brought Bebe?" Mr. Calhoun demanded, advancing on his wife. "Bebe knows, too? Why didn't you just tell the whole town while you were at it?"

"You've got Vince!" Mrs. Calhoun exclaimed right back. She poked her index finger into his chest. "You tell Vince before you tell me. Why shouldn't I tell my friend if my husband is cheating on me?"

"Actually," Bebe interjected smartly, "I was the one who saw you with the tootsie in the park, Mike." Her tight curls wiggled as she moved to back up her friend. "I was the one who, you know, put the pieces together. So Yvonne didn't tell me anything. I'm the one who told her."

"That's just great," Michael Calhoun spat. "Bebe is

running around making up stories and you believe her."

"She has pictures, Michael," Cooper's mother contended.

Bebe nodded. "Yeah, pictures."

"How could you, Michael?" Yvonne poked him in the chest again, harder this time. "How could you?"

"Mom?" Cooper stepped in between his parents. "Dad is not having an affair."

"Of course not," his father grumbled.

"Then what—?"

"It's a blackmail thing," Cooper explained cautiously.

His mother's eyebrows shot up. "Blackmail?"

Now it was Vince's turn to take center stage. Acting as if he'd just walked out of *Dragnet*, he said curtly, "Yeah, blackmail. Some story about Mike's love child." He sent Bebe a contemptuous glance. "I got pictures, too."

"Love child? She's having your baby?" Mrs. Calhoun cried. "That's even worse!"

"She's not having my baby," her husband shouted. "She's trying to convince me she *is* my baby."

"What?" Cooper's mother looked just about ready to faint, but she waved off Cooper, his father and Vince, all of whom rushed forward. "The tootsie in the park is your baby?"

"No, she's not."

"Maybe we should sit down," Cooper suggested.

"Hold on!" Yvonne Calhoun declared. "I think I've got it. You're not having an affair, Michael?"

"No affair?" Bebe asked sadly.

"Of course not!"

"But this girl, she says you had an affair way back when?" Mrs. Calhoun continued. "With her mother?"

"Yeah." He grimaced. "She says her mother was a con woman I had the goods on but didn't arrest so I could have sex with her. And Toni is supposedly the result. But it never happened, Yvonne, so don't even think—"

"Of course it didn't happen. I'm not that stupid, Mike. I know you would never have sex with some criminal, especially not back in the seventies. Sheesh. You were such a square back then. No way." Much calmer now, she patted her husband's arm. "So this tootsie is blackmailing you? She thinks she can get away with that?"

Her husband fixed her with hurt eyes. "I can't believe you thought I was having an affair."

"I can't believe you didn't tell me that little piece of trash was trying to blackmail you." Mrs. Calhoun was working herself into a lather again. "I'd like to throttle her with my bare hands."

Violet was starting to really like Cooper's mother.

She shook her head. "You should've told her to go jump in the lake. Who would believe her, anyway?"

"Stupid people who believe whatever they read in the paper," her husband grumbled.

"It could've been a real scandal," Vince said helpfully. "Mike wanted to head that off at the pass, you know, because of the promotion."

"Promotion, schmotion," his mother declared.

"Who cares if there's a scandal? You have to do what's right, which is to tell this blackmailer girl to stick her blackmail where the sun don't shine."

"Yvonne, I don't want to—"

"Mike, we need to put our heads together and take care of this," she interrupted. "She asked you for money, right?"

"Yeah, and she just doubled it because Coop shot some gumball machine."

Cooper held up a hand. "Don't even ask, Ma. I didn't shoot her gumball machine. And it's not important, anyway."

"So she squeezed you for money, it's already extortion and we can arrest her. Where is the drop supposed to be?" his mother inquired calmly.

Cooper narrowed his eyes. "What do you know about drops?"

"I haven't been married to a cop for thirty years for nothing. Besides, I watch TV," she said grandly.

"Noon," his dad responded. "She wants two hundred grand at noon, back in the park."

"So it's easy." Mrs. Calhoun brushed one hand against the other in a dismissive gesture. "Cooper, you go to the park at noon and you arrest that girl. You're a True Blue Calhoun, boy. You don't just look the other way when a crime is committed under your nose. Why, throwing this girl in the pokey might be enough to get you a meritorious promotion, too, like Sean got."

Violet gulped. Arrest Toni? Would Cooper go along with that?

He began to say, "Ma, I don't think—"

Meanwhile his dad warned, "Cooper shouldn't be—"

But his mother overrode them both. "That reminds me," she said, glancing around the room. "Bebe, did I leave my purse in your car? I need to call Sean and tell him that Cooper found the girl so he doesn't have to."

"You gonna tell Jake?" Vince whispered to his boss.

"Oh, yeah." The elder Calhoun looked gloomy. "I should let Jake know. I kind of...yelled at him the last time I talked to him. He told me he hadn't found Toni, and I was kind of steamed."

"It's all right, hon." His wife stood on tiptoe to give him a kiss on the cheek. "You were under a lot of stress."

All better now, apparently. All better for them, with secrets exposed and everyone on the same page. Everyone but Violet.

She watched Cooper's parents go separate ways in search of phones, and their friends toddle along after them, with everyone talking at once and disagreeing about just how the sting operation in the park should be handled. They agreed it was important to make sure the whole story—with the Deputy Superintendent and his sons hushing things up and carrying on their own investigation, not to mention a small bit of burglary and damage to property—stayed under wraps, but how they were to accomplish bringing Toni into custody as well as keeping her mouth shut was up in the air.

As well as minor details, like whether there should

be backup or not. Send Mike Calhoun with his son? Vince put his name in for consideration, and so did Bebe, but no, they went back to Cooper alone as the best choice in case Toni ran, since he was quicker. He could also create the least disturbance if he called in on-duty cops for help, but they also decided he should be sure to call for backup if he needed it.

Then they began to debate if Cooper should wear a wire to collect more proof.

Violet drank it all in, trying to come up with a plan of her own. She didn't want Toni arrested. But she didn't know how to stop the runaway train that was the Calhoun family in action.

All right then. Maybe her best choice was to slip away now, while she had the chance, show up at the park, too, and try to head Toni off before Cooper got there. Violet chewed the inside of her cheek. The ways things were going, the Calhouns would be calling in SWAT teams and helicopters and canine units. One little unauthorized FBI agent wasn't really going to be much of an obstruction.

She needed a plan. It was so hard to think with all this activity. *I have to get out of here.* Quietly rising from the sofa, she circled around outside the cluster of Calhouns and friends, edging closer to the front door.

"Wait a minute," Cooper called out. "Where are you going?"

Violet lunged for the door.

"Stop her!"

His father and Vince got there first, blocking her path. Damn it, anyway. She could feel Cooper coming up behind her, and he set a hand on her shoulder. She tried not to flinch, but she felt caught like a rat in a trap.

"Who are you?" Mr. Calhoun demanded.

"She was the girl on the sofa," Vince stated. "She was here when we got here."

"Yes, I know. But who is she?" He was staring right at Violet.

She opened her mouth. There was a long pause.

"She's my girlfriend," Cooper said finally. He looped an arm around her, pulling her back against his warm, bare chest, and then he dropped a kiss on the side of her neck. She felt a little funny all of a sudden. Hot and dizzy. *His girlfriend?*

"You got your girlfriend involved in this?" His dad looked upset all over again.

"Yeah, well, I couldn't help it," Cooper told him in a no-nonsense tone. He tucked her hand behind her back, hiding the handcuff with his own body, as he marched her back toward the sofa. "She kind of stumbled over it, so I had to tell her."

"Cooper has a girlfriend?" his mother asked in excitement. "And isn't she pretty? Cooper, why don't you have a shirt on, anyway? Why didn't you introduce the poor thing when we got here? She looks scared to death. What will she think of us?"

"It's fine. Really," Violet murmured.

Cooper shoved aside his duffel bag, sat down on the couch and pulled her with him. "Her name is Violet, Mom. Violet O'Leary."

"Are you related to the lady with the cow, the one

who started the Chicago Fire?" Yvonne Calhoun asked pleasantly. "Wouldn't that be funny?"

Cooper and his mother had one-track minds. Violet sent him a wry glance as she murmured, "No, I'm afraid I'm not from around here."

"And what do you do, hon?" his mom chirped, pulling up a comfy chair and inching in closer. "How old are you, Violet? How did you and my son meet each other?"

Her friend Bebe perched on the arm of her chair, as Vince and Cooper's dad hovered in the vicinity, shamelessly listening in. "Have you know each other long?" Bebe queried. "You have great hair. I'd love to get my hands on it. Maybe layer it a little."

"Bebe has a hair salon," Cooper whispered. He still had his arm around her, and he squeezed her closer.

Violet blinked, not really sure what to say or do. Sitting practically in Cooper's lap was bad enough, especially with him half-naked. But being bombarded with questions by his relatives? She'd been on the verge of escape, of getting back to her own life, the one where she was single-mindedly on Toni's trail, with no other distractions. Now she'd jumped into some crazy episode of "Meet the Parents." While he was half-dressed and she was wearing a handcuff.

Just when she'd thought things couldn't get any worse...

"So?" his mother prompted. "Let's hear the details. I'm so excited Cooper has a girlfriend. He's always been a little bit too much of a player to suit me. But you probably already knew that."

"No, I'm not a player and no, she didn't know that. So be quiet."

"Cooper, why don't you go put on a shirt?" Yvonne Calhoun suggested. "Let us girls talk."

"Oh, no, you don't," Violet said between gritted teeth.

Cooper kissed her again, this time on the cheek. "I'm not going anywhere, Vi. You're so cute to not want to be apart for even a second."

"Isn't it sweet?" Bebe cooed.

He turned to his mom. "She's twenty-eight, we met on the job, we haven't known each other very long, but it's been intense, and that's all I can think of. Want to add anything, Vi?"

"Nope. Not a thing," she said quickly.

"So she's an older woman." Mrs. Calhoun nodded sagely. "Very wise choice. A little more maturity is a step in the right direction for you, Cooper."

Violet felt this weird warm feeling in the pit of her stomach. Cooper's mother didn't mind that she was older than he was. *And she said I was pretty.* Considering the fact that she'd been up most of the night, she'd taken a five-minute shower, her clothes were rumpled, her hair was a mess and she had no makeup on whatsoever, that compliment was a real gift.

She couldn't believe it herself, but she heard, "Thank you so much, Mrs. Calhoun. It's a pleasure to meet you," come out of her mouth.

"And what did you say she did for a living?" This time it was his dad posing the question.

"I didn't," Cooper answered.

"Why not?" his father pressed. His expression was

dark and his eyes seemed to be focused on her thigh, where her wrist was hidden. Uh-oh. He'd seen the handcuff. "You said you met on the job. She's not a suspect, is she?"

Violet decided she could answer that one herself. "I'm an FBI agent, Mr. Calhoun." She didn't bother to explain the manacle. Let him think it was a sex toy. "Cooper was assigned to me as a contact for a particular case I was working on. That's how we met."

"An agent?" He arched an eyebrow, sending his son all kinds of messages and warnings without uttering a syllable.

"She's not after Toni," Cooper mumbled. "She's not a problem here, Dad." Only Violet knew he was lying through his teeth. For her.

"Wow, that's an exciting job. Cooper, this girl is perfect for you," Mrs. Calhoun gushed. "I love her already."

Violet couldn't help the small smile that played over her lips. Clearly, Cooper took more after his mother than his father. Barrel right ahead, take no prisoners, don't even notice the existence of obstacles.... She liked this woman.

Cooper stood up, moving in front of her. "Look, Mom, Violet and I were up half the night, uh, working on the case. We're both really tired. So why don't we do this some other time, okay?"

"I just met her," his mother protested.

"Yes, I know, but I promise Violet and I will come by for Sunday dinner or whatever you want. Quality time," he vowed.

Violet had to hand it to him; he did have a knack

for lying and making it sound good. Up half the night working on the case? Bringing his girlfriend by for Sunday dinner? Not even one bit of truth to any of it. She shook her head. She was almost sorry she was never going to make that Sunday dinner at the Calhoun house.

"What about Toni and the park?" his father asked in a dire undertone.

"I'm on it. I will be there at noon. As soon as she mentions the two hundred thou, I'll arrest her right then for the extortion and the credit card fraud and the rest of it." He set his jaw. "She's not getting past me this time."

Violet felt a sinking feeling in the pit of her stomach. He sounded as if he meant it. *I'll arrest her right then. She's not getting past me this time....*

"Okay, everybody. Out," Cooper ordered. "Violet and I need some sleep so we can be fresh for our little sting in the park."

It took a few minutes to get rid of them, and she definitely heard his mother chiding his father for giving "the kids" a hard time when they obviously wanted to be alone, with a wink and everything. Finally, they were all gone. Cooper locked the door behind them, then threw the dead bolt. He wasn't taking any chances, was he?

Violet rubbed her eyes. Man, she was tired. She really wished some of this made sense. She had tough decisions to make, and she didn't want any part of them.

When Cooper walked back over to where she still sat on the sofa, she gazed up him thoughtfully. "Cooper, why did you tell them I was your girlfriend?"

10

"WHY?" he murmured in a teasing tone. He reached down and took her right hand in his, bringing it up to his lips, letting the handcuffs jingle in the air. "Well, darling, you *are* wearing my bracelet. Doesn't that make us half-engaged?"

"Half-insane is more like it." She pretended she was going to clonk him with the free end of it.

"Look, Violet, I'm sorry about the handcuff thing. I should never have taken unfair advantage like that, and I want to apologize." Still hanging on to her hand, he was acting all humble and earnest, and she had no idea if it was an act or not. "Okay? Will you accept my apology?"

"Do you mean that?"

"Absolutely." He pressed his lips to the back of her hand again, sending her a smoky glance before brushing tiny kisses all around her wrist inside the circle of the cuff.

She hated how easy it was for him to get past her defenses. But how could she resist? When he turned it on, he could toast her like a marshmallow over an open flame. Now if she only knew whether she could trust him. Once burned...

"About the handcuffs..." She licked her lip.

Cooper raised his head from her hand, and she could see the spark of interest there. "What about them?"

"I have to admit, it was kind of sexy in a twisted way. I'm not used to *twisted* being a good thing." She tried to laugh, but it came out sounding sort of choked. "But it was kind of intriguing, if you know what I mean."

"I can do twisted," he said quickly.

"First, though..." She tugged on his hand, pulling him closer to where she sat on the couch. "I'm afraid you're injured, Cooper. I think we should take a look at those ribs."

"I'm not..." he started, but broke off when her lips met his skin, right above his belly button.

"How did that feel?" She feigned innocence, fluttering her eyelashes as she looked up at him. "Any pain?"

"Uh, yeah. Some."

"That's not good." Kicking off her shoes, she yanked him down onto the sofa, pushing him backward, climbing on top. As she bent over him, she moved ever so slowly, pretending to assess the damages, but unsnapping the top button on his jeans. She opened them just a quarter of an inch, exposing a bit more skin than she'd intended. Oh, yeah. He wasn't wearing anything under there. Better slow down.

She had to remember to keep breathing, to stay on course here. This time *he* was going to be the one swimming in a sea of desire, not her. So she took her hands off his fly, not exactly trusting herself.

Instead, she ran her palms over his hard, muscled

chest. The handcuff trailed over his flat stomach, and she knew the steel must feel cold against his warm skin. He jumped. Good.

"I think," she murmured in her throatiest purr, "you're a bit tender here...." She dropped a kiss on his breastbone. "And maybe here..." She dipped lower.

"I think you're right," he whispered with a smile, lying back and giving her free rein.

Violet wiggled just a little, completely on top of him now, tracing a path from his shoulder to his belt with her moist lips and tongue. She could feel his heart pounding in his chest, and he was breathing more heavily. She smiled with satisfaction. She had him right where she wanted him.

She unzipped another inch.

"I thought you didn't want to see me out of my pants," he said, and his voice was husky and uneven.

Violet gazed up and down the beautiful expanse of his sun-bronzed body, to the top of his jeans, where the hard ridge of his desire strained against the heavy denim. The hell with it. "I changed my mind." She put her finger on the tab of his zipper, eager to drag it down the rest of the way.

But Cooper fooled her. Raising up a fraction, he tumbled both of them off the couch and onto the floor, bracing her with his body. And now he was on top, still wearing his jeans. With his knees at her hips, he leaned down to rub his cheek against her hair, to trace the outline of her ear with his tongue, to slip one hand under the edge of her T-shirt, to explore whatever he wanted to explore, safely holding his hips far enough away.

"No fair," she argued, arching up into him as his hand curved around her breast. But her body was responding and they both knew it.

"I'm into fairness. Like you and me wearing the same amount of clothes," he said roughly. It took him about a second to slide her shirt and the tank top she'd worn under it safely out of his way, bunching the fabric above her breasts, exposing her naked flesh completely to his hot gaze.

There was nothing she could do but hang on and try to remember to breathe, as he bent to take her eager nipples into his mouth, laving them and tweaking them with his tongue and his teeth. As she writhed under him, he slid the length of his bare torso down hers, rubbing his chest against her breasts, undoing her pants, pushing them down. Her gasp of pleasure seemed to inflame him even more, and he tried to peel her T-shirt and bra off over her head to get rid of them altogether. But he got stuck when he hit the handcuff.

"Aw, damn it." Momentarily distracted, he rammed a hand into his jeans pocket, coming up with a small silver key. That was all it took. As she watched, nonplussed, he unlocked the handcuff and tossed it aside, smoothly pulling off her bunched-up shirt and lingerie at the same time.

"Wait a minute. You had the key this whole time?"

"Well, since I got home. I had a spare." With the key tucked back in his pocket, he lay on his side, pulling her to him, ready to take up where he'd left off.

Violet held him back with her hand flat against his chest. "You had a spare and you waited this long to tell me?"

"It didn't hurt anything." Intent on what he was doing, he had somehow managed to maneuver her pants the rest of the way off over her hips and past her knees, while she was still back on the issue of the key.

And now she was at a decided disadvantage, wearing nothing but a tiny pair of blue thong panties, while he was still in his jeans. Besides, she couldn't really concentrate on being cranky or being in charge while his hands roamed over her breasts and her bottom, causing all sorts of maddening sensations. One hand curved around her buttock, pressing her up and in, so that her pelvis rode hard against his. With the other, he hooked a finger under the thin band of ribbon at the top of her thong, tugging on the fabric.

The insistent pressure on a vulnerable spot from two different directions was driving her insane. She tried to grab at his hands, but she was already rocking with his rhythm, and he just batted her away, continuing the exquisite torture. Wiggling enough to rid herself of the pants tangled around her ankles, she eased right back into that sweet spot, raising her knee, angling herself even closer, moaning with the perfection of it.

Cooper captured her mouth then, swirling his tongue into hers, delving deeper, driving her with the same pulsing beat that pounded in her loins. She couldn't breathe, didn't care if she ever breathed again, as long as this overwhelming need consumed her. Sensation curled inside her, already starting to unspool.

But Cooper pulled back. "Let's slow this down," he whispered. Tangling his hands in her long, dark curls, he dotted slow, sweet kisses on her cheeks and her forehead, running his hands gently over her shoulders and her spine, up her thigh and down her calf, barely dancing over her stomach and her breasts, making her flush as he murmured soft words. "You're beautiful, Violet. And your skin feels amazing. I've never seen a woman with such gorgeous skin. I just can't stop touching you."

It was delicious to feel so loved and cherished, and Violet relaxed under his caresses. Still, that brief moment returned enough air and enough sense to her brain to remind her that things were not supposed to be proceeding this way. She had no intention of coming apart at the seams with him so far behind. Again. This time, he would be the one who lost control.

"Let's take this game into the bedroom," she suggested, breathing her words into his ear. Her voice came out all wispy and weird, but she knew he heard her when he sat back and offered her a hand. "And don't forget the handcuffs."

Cooper smiled, with that familiar spark of mischief lighting his blue, blue eyes. Without a word, he snagged the handcuffs and Violet at the same time, taking them both quickly down the hall into his bedroom.

She sized up the possibilities. As in the living room, he'd gone for simple furnishings, with dark wood and white fabrics. His bed was made, so a gold star for Cooper for that, with a thick down comforter tossed over plain white linens that looked just right for sinking into. Better yet, he had a headboard with horizontal wooden slats running all the way across. Perfect for her purposes.

Hang on, Violet, she told herself. *You can do it, girl.*

He dropped the handcuffs onto the bedside table as she eased herself into the bed. And then he slid in beside her.

"Maybe you should get rid of the jeans," she told him shyly.

"Maybe you should get rid of them for me."

She swallowed. He had to be naked. He had to. Besides, the key was still in the pocket of those jeans. But her hand was shaking as she edged down his zipper, a little, a little more, until she could see all of him. And just how much he wanted her. Her mouth watered.

Her good intentions were disappearing into thin air. Biting her lip as she concentrated, she backed off the side of the bed, dragging his jeans down his legs, tossing them into the hallway.

Cooper was still smiling, but the light of mischief in his eyes had blossomed into flame. "Violet," he said, reaching for her, "why are you over there when I'm over here?"

"I'm coming," she murmured, climbing back on, looming over him on all fours. Her hair spilled over her shoulders and around her face, silken tendrils sliding across his chest, just brushing his hipbone, grazing his erection, making it jerk like a puppet on a string as she swished her hair back and forth.

"Don't ever cut your hair," he whispered.

Violet smiled. Her hand closed around his rigid shaft, stroking gently, and he swore under his breath, something pithy and dark. Her smile widened as she bent even closer, touching just the tip of her tongue to the tip of him, not releasing her grip.

Cooper groaned. "Holy... Violet, this may be over fast if you keep that up."

But she had no intention of letting go. She took more of him between her lips and deeper into her mouth, swirling her tongue around, getting used to the intimate taste and feel of Cooper, steely hard, velvety soft and pulsing with energy, slipping him in and out as she stroked him with her fingers.

"Violet," he warned, "oh, Lord..."

She knew he was getting close, for his pulse quickened under her hand. She picked up her pace, pushing him to come to her.

"Unh-uh," he growled.

Once again, when she thought she had things under control, he pounced. Air rushed out of her in a whoosh as he rolled out from under her and pinned her on her stomach in one powerful motion.

"It's not supposed to work like that," she said angrily, trying to raise her head. It was impossible with Cooper lying on top of her, crushing her into the bed. Somehow a pillow had gotten stuck under her stomach, and she could feel his hard length prodding her bottom from behind. Attempting to get up, she wiggled against his stiff, unyielding flesh, inadvertently bringing herself to shocked, wet arousal in the space of two seconds. She didn't want to want him this badly. She wanted to make him want *her*. She felt like weeping with the injustice of it. But she couldn't stop squirming with need. "I wanted to—"

"I know what you wanted. Maybe next time."

Behind her, above her, Cooper looped an arm under her to lift her hips from the pillow, stripping off her baby-blue thong with his other hand. She tried to resist, but all she managed to do was thrash ineffectually as Cooper knelt between her thighs from behind.

His knees pushed hers apart, making a wide V that he nudged into, edging himself closer to her hot, moist core.

As she tipped forward, Violet's hands fisted in the sheets. Cooper filled her, thrust easily inside her, shallow and then deep, slow and then fast. The pace he was setting was tantalizing, torturous, as he slammed himself into her and then withdrew, making her quiver and shake to take him deeper again. She arched back into him as best she could, desperate to find the rhythm.

His body was glazed with sweat, his chest slippery against her back, and he skated his hands over her, caressing and kneading her breasts and her belly, edging lower, threading through her curls to flick and rub his thumb against her sensitive nub. That small, persistent motion sent her soaring immediately. There was no way for her to hold back as waves of hard, shuddering release swept her.

"Cooper, Cooper," she cried out. It was the only word her brain could form, but it was more of an urgent plea than an endearment, as if she were begging him not to let her go, not to stop, not to let it end.

He had her in a fierce, relentless grip, pumping into her, rasping over her, and she came again, hard on the heels of the first time, shattering into a million pieces, as he plunged to his own explosive climax.

She was dizzy and weak, still feeling reverberations as they both collapsed into the pillows.

"Oh, my God," she whispered. That was not supposed to happen. Not like this.

"That was the most fabulous thing I've ever done in my life," he mumbled, hauling her onto his chest as he fell back into the sheets. "I'm exhausted. And yet I want to do it again. Your way this time. Any way. Every way." His arms tightened and he dropped a kiss onto her hair. He sounded as surprised as she felt when he said, "Violet, I may never be able to let you go."

Violet tried not to panic. But she felt exactly the same way. Exhausted, alive, her whole body hummed with satisfaction even as it told her it was already greedy for another go.

I may never be able to let you go.

It wasn't supposed to be like this! Now what was she going to do?

The bedside clock glowed at her, mocking her: 8:00 a.m. She had four hours to decide what to do. Betray Cooper and his family? Or her own? Fall back and allow herself to be a slave to lust? Or admit that there was more than mere lust happening here?

Her eyes focused on the clock. Four hours.

COOPER AWOKE WITH A START, not sure where he was or why his body ached in so many different places. It was light in his bedroom, and the bedside clock read 11:00 a.m., so why was he asleep? Then he saw the blue-violet, dark-lashed eyes staring down at him, and it all came back. In Technicolor. "Violet," he murmured, reaching for her. She was sort of leaning across him, plenty close for him to get to anything he wanted.

"Cooper?" She sounded surprised. "I thought you were still asleep."

"Time to get up," he responded drowsily. Past time. Especially if he wanted to work in one more little romp before he had to go to the park to bring down Toni. As he ran his hands over Violet's bottom, as usual bare except for the string of that damn thong underwear she always wore, he felt a familiar reaction down below. Something was definitely up. Violet had a habit of making that happen.

Surely they had time to squeeze in some fun. Maybe in the shower. Then they could combine items on the schedule and he wouldn't lose any time. Well, not much time.

The thong was white, when he could've sworn the thing he'd peeled off her a few hours ago was a different color. She also had on a matching white tank top. And her hair looked wet.

That was a lot more clothing than he actually preferred her to be in.

"Cooper?" she asked again, but her tone had changed this time. Now she sounded more naughty and teasing. She let her wet hair drip on his bare chest, and then bent over far enough to lick up the drop. "Are you ready to wake up now?"

The second she touched her tongue to his skin he could feel his manhood rising up like a good little soldier to greet her, tenting the sheet at his lap. "I guess you already took a shower," he murmured, trying to maneuver her nearer to the ache in his groin. "I thought we might do that together."

"In a minute maybe. If I get dirty again." She smiled. "Why don't you just lie back and let me take care of you?"

"What exactly does that mean, Violet?" he asked suspiciously, raising himself up on one elbow.

But she didn't answer, just whipped his sheet away, leaving him all uncovered and gloriously erect, as she scooted to the bottom of the bed. She slid her hands over his ankles.

"Starting down there, huh?"

"Uh-huh. I thought I might lick my way to the top," she said huskily, gazing up at him with heavy-lidded, sultry violet eyes.

Cooper took a deep breath. He wasn't sure how patient he was going to be. Not just because of the stupid errand, but because he felt a certain undeniable hunger rising.

But then he heard the clink of metal and felt the chill of steel around his ankle. He sat up in time to see her hook the other cuff around a slat in the footboard. "Oh, yeah. I got so caught up in the way we were doing it before, I forgot the handcuffs," he declared, lying back, grinning. "Of course, I thought you were going to be the one who got tied up."

"I know you did. But I wanted to surprise you." She slithered up his body, offering a sensual promise he couldn't wait to hold her to as she reached over his head, her breasts bobbing behind that camisole at just about eye level.

There was no way he was going to ignore that invitation. He skated his hands under her top, enjoying the smooth, soft feel of her ivory skin, homing in on her full, luscious breasts and those tempting, hard little peaks.

But she tugged one hand off her breast, stretching his arm up to the headboard.

"Aw, you're no fun," he grumbled.

And another handcuff snapped into place, binding him securely.

"Where did you get the extra handcuffs?" he inquired, already thinking up ways to get around that impediment if Violet would just stay put.

"The trunk of my car," she said tersely. She jumped out of the bed.

He had a bad feeling about this all of a sudden. "I thought we were past that," he tried. "Are you still holding a grudge?"

"Oh, we're past round one." She folded her arms over her chest, giving him a determined smile. "Now we're in the middle of round two. I'm up at bat."

"That's innings, not rounds."

"I'm still at bat." She pulled on her pants.

"Point taken. And I know, now that your point has been made, you're going to let me go. Think about it, Violet. You were mad because you came and I didn't. Well, this time we both got to where we needed to go," he argued. "Nobody finished alone. Although you're still ahead on points."

"I know." She edged in closer, dropping a sweet, short kiss onto his lips. "It really was great, Cooper, and I really would love to stick around."

"Stick around?" he echoed uneasily. Wasn't that what he'd said, just before he, uh, left her, securely manacled to the bed?

"You see, I'm going to meet up with Toni in the park in your place, and I don't want you horning in on my collar," she said mockingly, echoing his words from before. She pulled a fitted white T-shirt on over her head and smoothed it down over her pants. "Don't worry. As soon as I take care of Toni, I'll come back. Shouldn't take more than a few hours. And then we can pick up where we left off." She stepped back to rake her gaze over him from top to bottom, from his shackled wrist, down over the peaks and valleys of his long, lean body, all the way to his shackled foot. "I gotta tell you. This pose looks amazing on you."

"Violet..."

But she was gone, twitching her little hips and sashaying right out of his house.

Watching her go, Cooper was almost admiring. After the morning they'd just spent, he would've been willing to let her lash him to any bed, anytime.

Of course, it also helped that he was a whiz when it came to getting out of handcuffs. If he could just reach that paper clip on the bedside table...

11

It took longer than he'd expected to get himself out of those stupid handcuffs. The extrication process was complicated by the fact that there were two of them, that it wasn't easy jiggling the paper clip over his head, and that her set of cuffs was slightly different from his.

That was life with Violet. Always complications.

Cooper wasn't too worried. He knew the city a lot better than she did, meaning it should be quicker for him to avoid the usual traffic problems, road repair and slow cross streets to get up to Humboldt Park. He still expected to be only minutes behind her when push came to shove. Plenty of time to round up Toni and spirit her out of FBI custody before she blabbed or made more of a nuisance of herself than she already had.

Of course, he had forgotten that they'd left his car on the edge of Lake View, near Toni's apartment, and nowhere near his neighborhood, so he had to catch a train and walk six blocks just to pick up the Jeep. So much for arriving only minutes behind her.

He could see the seconds ticking away on his watch. Great. Way to go, getting bamboozled and outplayed by Violet. Letting the entire Calhoun family down.

But when he arrived at the park, cautiously heading for the spot his father had specified, he stopped in his tracks. There they were, Violet and Toni, sitting calmly on a bench, talking.

Talking? They looked like old friends. This was not what he'd expected.

As he watched, they actually hugged each other. Both of them looked a little teary, and Violet handed Toni a tissue. They hugged again, longer this time, and then Violet reached for that big old shoulder bag. She rooted around for a while, pulled out a roll of bills, handed the whole wad to Toni, who took the money.

"Violet is paying her off? Why?" Cooper was absolutely mystified.

He'd figured there was more to Violet tracking Toni than FBI business, given that she was on her own, clearly not following regulations and more than a bit secretive. But he'd figured that meant she had a personal vendetta. Not a personal relationship.

If he'd known that Violet was handing over money, he would've said that Toni was playing more extortion games, that she had something on Vi. But Violet didn't look as if anyone was putting the screws to her. This looked like a voluntary thing. Like a gift, maybe.

And why would Violet O'Leary be making lavish gifts to Toni Jones?

Cooper considered the interplay between them. Hugging. Touching. Crying. They sure looked like old pals now.

He tried to remember how they'd behaved when they'd seen each other at the apartment, but all he could recall was Violet telling everyone to freeze and Toni screeching about her door. Not exactly a heart-felt reunion.

So how did this tearful meeting in the park add up? Frankly, as far as he could tell, it didn't.

"Oh, hell."

After one last hug, Toni was backing away from the park bench, mouthing "Thank you, thank you" over and over again.

Cooper muttered, "She can't be letting her walk away."

And yet she was. What was Violet thinking? A federal officer aiding and abetting, maybe even getting in on the conspiracy? This kind of nonsense could get her pretty butt canned.

Cooper had another issue with this new wrinkle, too. Where exactly did Violet expect Toni to escape to? Somewhere she could hide out and plot new blackmail games against his family or someone else's? Another hotel to rip off or credit cards to steal? He should never have tried to get her out of town and given her a free pass in the first place. And he did not plan to make that mistake twice.

Nope. No way was Toni walking. Not this time.

He had the green light to arrest her, after all. And there were plenty of charges piling up, maybe even including whatever she had going with Violet. Time to stop fooling around and treating Toni like some-one special. Time to call in the troops, just to be sure the odds were in his favor.

As he tracked Toni through the park, Cooper pulled out his cell phone and muttered the requisite info to a dispatcher. He stuck the phone back in his pocket, circling around behind a tree to step right in the center of Toni's path.

"Hey, Toni. What's up?"

"Oh, man," she spat. "Not you again."

"Yeah, I'm real happy to see you, too." Cooper took her arm, yanking her back toward the bench where Violet still sat. Toni kept swearing at him and trying to get away, but Cooper was in no mood to be messed with. He didn't even speak to her, just grabbed her purse, took the money Violet had given her and stuffed it in his own pocket.

He had no handcuffs—his were still attached to his headboard back at the house—and he sorely missed them right now. Handcuffs and a gag would've been really handy. Yeah, the more she whined and moaned, the more he realized that Toni was someone he would definitely like to chain up in a cell somewhere. Somewhere he wasn't.

As for Violet...

"Cooper." She said his name with no emotion whatsoever, but her eyes were huge and troubled. "I was actually waiting for you, Cooper. I knew you'd get here sooner or later." She paused before adding, "I just didn't expect you to have Toni with you."

"Yeah, well, I've acted stupid about this long enough." He dumped her cash in her lap. "I should've arrested her as soon as she left the hotel."

"Gimme a break," Toni muttered. She plumped herself onto the bench next to Violet. "Vi, you can make this go away, can't you? I need a new start, that's all. You said so, too."

Violet didn't answer. She was gazing at Cooper with a mixture of regret and defiance. On her, it looked beautiful, but then, what didn't?

He was out of patience at this point. "Okay, Vi, spill," he commanded. "I want to hear it from you. Why are you paying her off? Is she blackmailing you, too? But why so chummy?"

"It's really simple, Cooper. Yes, she deserves to do the time for what she's done, but..." She chewed her lip. "She can't go to jail again. She's this close to doing hard time."

"Maybe because she deserves it?"

"Yes, but if she can go somewhere and start over, stop the blackmail and the petty scams—you know, become the person she could be—I know it will be all right." She took his hand and squeezed it, imploring him. "Please, Cooper?"

Right before his eyes, Violet had turned into someone he didn't recognize. "Vi, this isn't you. I know you." He ran a hand through his hair, totally taken aback. "You are law and order down to your toes. What the heck is going on? A little bait and switch?"

"It's not like that," Violet insisted, but Toni cut her off, getting in Cooper's face.

"You think you know her? For how long? A couple of days?" Toni scoffed. "Well, I've known her forever. Her whole life. Can you beat that, Calhoun?"

Her whole life? Just what the hell were these two to each other?

She continued, with the same self-righteous overtones, "And Violet is smart and damn good at her job, too, but that doesn't mean she doesn't have a heart. She has feelings. She knows about love. Unlike some people. Damn Calhouns. I never should've gotten involved with you heartless jerks."

"Involved with?" He arched an eyebrow. "Is that what you're calling blackmail now?"

"It doesn't change the fact that you don't know her like I do," she insisted. "Face it, you're nothing to Violet. But we've been tight our whole lives. We're there for each other. She knows I am in love and just married and I deserve a chance. People in love deserve a chance."

"She's known you your whole life?" Cooper demanded. That was the second time she'd said that. "What the heck is going on here?"

Violet said quietly, "Toni, you haven't known me my whole life."

"Almost."

"Not even close."

"Violet, I am trying to defend you here. Cut me a break!" Toni protested.

This time Cooper interrupted. He just couldn't stand there and let her play on Violet's sympathies that way. "Toni, you're trying to save your own sorry butt, not defend her. You're playing her like she's another mark." He took on a mocking tone. "'Violet, you're so smart. Violet, you have a heart. I'm in love. Violet will give me another chance.' I know a con when I hear one, even if Violet doesn't."

"I do, but…" Ignoring Toni, Violet tried again with Cooper. "Just this once, turn the other way. Let her go. It's what you and your father wanted before. I know you want her gone as much as I do."

"And why is that, Violet? Why do you want her gone?" His tone was implacable. "Why are you two so tight?"

"Cooper, she's my sister."

His jaw dropped. Her *sister*?

He didn't have a clue how to deal with that information, but it didn't matter. He heard sirens. His backup was there. Too late to make choices about Toni now. It was out of his hands. "Violet, put the money away," he ordered her under his breath.

His brothers in blue were on the scene in no time, ready to haul away Toni on the information Cooper had already phoned in about the hotel and the credit card theft. Ignoring the sick feeling in the pit of his stomach—Toni was Violet's *sister*?—Cooper went on automatic pilot, filling them in on the pertinent details about possible other charges and jurisdictional issues until Toni decided it was time to stop being polite.

She tried to run, got hauled back and then started to yell her head off. "Listen, my sister is a Fed, okay? I—I been undercover for her, trying to catch someone more important. And she is not going to let you people arrest me like this. Tell them, Violet."

Violet opened her mouth, but closed it again.

"Vi, are you going to let them take me away?" Toni screamed, kicking and smacking at the officers.

"Okay, now we got you for resisting," the larger of the two policemen grumbled, unimpressed with her histrionics. To Cooper, he announced, "We'll catch up with the rest of the paperwork later, Calhoun. Come down to the station and we'll figure out where she needs to go and who gets her first."

"Yeah, fine." He didn't care which charges they booked her on or even where they did it, but attempted extortion of the Calhoun family was going into the mix.

"You are a sucker, Violet!" Toni snarled as her parting shot. "I was never going to repent and try your lily-white life. Yeah, right. Like I want to live like a chump. I like my life fine, Vi. You just remember that!"

Violet had her head in her hands as they led her sister away.

"Well, you had the chance to lie, to say it was a sting or something. You could've waltzed off with her, Vi." Cooper sat down beside her. "You didn't."

"Yeah, I know. I finally did the right thing," she said bitterly.

"Yes, actually, you did. You heard her. You weren't doing her any favors letting her go."

"I know, but…"

"But she's your sister," he finished for her. "Blood is thicker than water. Yeah, I know."

Violet fiddled with the strap of her shoulder bag. "She's my half sister," she said quietly. "We have the same father. Mr. Jones, not Mr. O'Leary. He, uh, was a con man. I only met him once. Remember when you asked me if there was a Mr. O'Leary and I said no, never?" Her lips twisted in a sad smile. "I wasn't lying."

He didn't know what to say. His heart ached for Violet. Okay, so she'd done some stupid things today. But it wasn't like he was perfect. And this bit about her father... Cooper couldn't imagine that was pleasant, for someone as honest as Violet to deal with the idea that she had a con man for a father.

Violet went on describing him, looking down at her hands. "My mom said he was very handsome and very charming. But not a nice person. That's what she said. Handsome and charming, but not a nice person."

Ah. So that explained her difficulties with trust issues. Cooper relied on charm and Violet was averse to charm. He'd need to make a note of that. The games of cross and double-cross they'd been playing must've driven her nuts. "So you and Toni didn't grow up together," he guessed.

"Nope. I didn't even know about her till I was sixteen. My mother is really sweet and she thinks family is important." She sighed. "I was an only child so she was just sure I would want to know my sister." Her voice dropped another notch, and he had to lean closer to hear her. "I guess her mother was my father's partner in crime. Toni grew up in the family biz, you could say, whereas my mom was a schoolteacher. So, you know, if you're assigning blame..."

"Vi, it's not your fault," he told her, taking her hand, pulling it between both of his. "She had a messed-up life. A lot of kids do. But you can't fix that for her now."

But Violet pulled her hand away. She straightened, sounding much more businesslike and brusque all of a sudden. "She has had various aliases, by the way, some of which you know about. I've been tracking her for a while. So, you know, I can provide anything you need in the way of victim statements, as well as photos of the gumball machine, which, of course, isn't around anymore."

"That's fine, Vi. We'll take care of that later."

"I'll be happy to do anything I can to help prosecute this expeditiously." She nodded, lifting her chin. "I have quite a file on her. So maybe that will, you know, take some of the pressure off your family as far as laying the whole blackmail mess on the line. We could just go with the gumballs. But that means she'll get nailed by the Feds. We really do have federal jurisdiction on the gumball scam."

"Speaking of federal jurisdiction..." he began. It was something he'd been wondering about for a while. "Does the Bureau know you're here, Violet? Are you going to be in big trouble for this?"

"I, um, had tacit approval. Unofficially." Awkwardly, she turned to him, speeding up as she explained, "I have a very good job record and this was something I really wanted to handle. The gumball scam, I mean. I knew it was Toni. I hadn't seen her in years. So, off the record, my boss said okay. Of course, I didn't tell him I was going to decide to encourage her to flee or give her money or screw everything up in such a, um, *huge* manner, but... What can you do?"

"Violet," he chided, getting tired of her beating herself up. This was not the fiery, ferocious competitor he knew. "You should've told me. I understand family loyalty. We could've worked together."

"Okay, I need to point out two things," she said darkly. "One, you didn't tell me, either, until this morning when I overheard a bunch of stuff. And two, your family is worth your loyalty, Cooper. I've met your parents and their friends, and they're all so cool. So normal. I can understand wanting to protect them. Anyone would. But my family... Except for my mother, mine isn't worth my loyalty. I jeopardized my career for her. For nothing!"

Good. She was starting to get angry. As far as he was concerned, it was a very healthy sign. "Yeah, but you had to try." He shrugged, looping an arm around her. "That's family for you. Drives you nuts, but you just keep trying."

And speaking of family...

His parents had just arrived. He happened to glance up and there they were, scurrying across the grass. Great. Just what he needed at this moment.

"Cooper!" his father yelled from yards away, approaching on the double, hand in hand with his mother. Okay, the hand-holding thing was a new wrinkle. And no Vince or Bebe this time, but Cooper figured it was only a matter of time.

Cooper noticed that Violet sat up straighter as his parents joined them. "Batten down the hatches," he muttered so only she could hear. "We're in for a storm."

"Here's the deal," his father said, launching into a rundown without bothering with any preliminaries. "I just got the call that she's been arrested and she's bringing up my name and yours all over the place, spilling her lies. What the hell did you do, Coop? Just how bad did you screw it up?"

"He didn't screw anything up," Violet protested. "It's not Cooper's fault."

"All due respect, miss. But he's my son," Mike Calhoun said with a frown.

"It's okay, Vi," Cooper offered lightly. "He's right about this one. I am a screwup. Always have been, right, Dad?"

Violet blinked. "A screwup? That's really stupid, Cooper. You did some fine police work here. Well, all except for excessive handcuffing."

He tried not to cough. "Let's not bring that up right now, okay?" he muttered.

"The bottom line is that you found Toni. Neither of your brothers, not your dad, not Vince, not your mom, not Bebe. You found her, Cooper." Violet's voice got louder and more confident. "You even killed her gumball machine, so now she can't be pulling the old gumball scam on unsuspecting merchants. In fact, I'm thinking you should apply to the FBI. I could, uh, recommend you."

"The FBI?" his father echoed doubtfully.

"Yes," Violet repeated. "I think he would be great."

Mrs. Calhoun joined in. "Violet is right, Mike. It's not Cooper's fault. All that sneaking around you did. I'm ashamed of you, blaming Cooper for your mistakes."

"I asked him for one simple thing, Yvonne. One simple thing. Jake could've done it."

"Don't be bringing up Jake," his wife snapped.

"Jake's not even here and we don't know where he is. You make me so mad when you do that. Poor Cooper!"

Cooper rose from the bench, meeting his father's gaze. He was tired of letting his mother and his girlfriend speak for him. Even though he had to say Violet's stirring defense made him feel pretty good. Was she serious about the G-man thing? He'd have to ask her when they were alone. He glanced at her. She really thought he'd done some fine police work? Violet just kept surprising him.

But first, he had to deal with his father. "Look, Dad, I tried. She wasn't going to keep her mouth shut, no matter what we did. And I have to tell you, it never should've gotten this far. Mom is right. You never should've taken her threats seriously, and you just should've outed her from the get-go."

"But your mother," his father argued. "And the press. My promotion. I couldn't."

"Yeah, well, you should've." Cooper took Violet by the hand, drawing her away from the park bench and his parents. "Excuse us, okay? We're still a little short on sleep. This has been kind of an ordeal."

"Listen to that. They're out on their feet, the poor things. And you, Michael, giving them a hard time. What's the matter with you?" Yvonne smacked her husband on the shoulder, and he just glowered at her. Rolling her eyes, she turned to her son, kissing him fondly on the cheek. "Cooper, honey, you take Violet and get her something to eat, and then you two get some sleep. And ignore your father. It will all work out. You'll see. We're the True Blue Calhouns. Nothing beats us."

"Thanks, Mom." He kissed her, too, hoping she was right, pretty sure she wasn't. But one way or the other, they would all muddle through. And maybe, just maybe, he would apply to the FBI Academy. Why not?

As he dealt with his mother, he noticed Violet trying to sneak behind him under the radar. But Yvonne Calhoun wasn't going for that.

"Violet, hon, you look so pale. Make sure Cooper takes you to get something to eat, okay?" She patted her on the arm. "I know he never keeps any food in that house of his, so be sure to stop on the way. And if not, come by my house, because I'm stocked. Do you cook, Violet?"

Cooper was going to save her from that one, but realized he was actually curious about it himself.

"I, uh...well, a little," she admitted. "I like desserts."

"Excellent." This time his mother didn't just pat her, she squeezed her. "You're going to be such a welcome addition to the family. I make a mean piecrust myself. And I have more cookie recipes than you can shake a stick at."

"Okay." Violet smiled, and Cooper clasped her hand in his. He could tell she was a little flummoxed by his mom. But, hey, who wasn't?

Since he and Violet hadn't really talked about any of that "addition to the family" stuff—they hadn't really talked about anything—he regarded her a little warily as he walked her back to her car. What did she think was her next move? Would it be out of Chicago and back to wherever it was she came from? There were so many things he didn't know about her, so many things he was dying to find out. Would he get the chance?

She glanced up at him. "Are you coming with me? Are you willing to let me drive and, uh, ride together?"

"Is that an invitation?"

Violet licked her lip. "Maybe."

"Okay. You can drive."

Violet nodded. She seemed thoughtful as they drove back south, toward his neighborhood. The funny thing was that neither actually asked where they were going; they just knew.

Food was a whole different issue that took a good deal of wrangling. Finally, with some deli stuff and some nice bread and condiments spread out on his kitchen table, Violet came back to what he knew she would eventually.

"Should we have let your mother think that I'm going to be around?" she asked delicately. "I mean, with the cookie recipes and all? I realize that she is your mom, and you know how to handle her, so maybe later you can just say, oh, we broke up. But she's so nice, and I like her a lot, and I feel bad lying to her. About us."

"Who says we're lying?"

"Oh, come on! We barely know each other." She piled some more turkey on her rye bread. "I don't even know how many days because it's been such a blur, but it's not long. So we're hardly, you know, a couple."

"I know you a heck of a lot better than any other girlfriend I've ever had," he said flatly. "Deal with it, Violet. We're totally a couple."

"We are not."

"Yeah, we are." He leaned over the table, snagging the last pickle off her plate. "The thing is, Violet, I'm pretty sure I'm in love with you."

She choked on her bite of sandwich. Without a word, Cooper handed her a glass of water. She wheezed for a bit, tapping her chest, but he wasn't fooled by that stalling technique.

"Come on, Violet. You can't be that surprised. It isn't every girl I handcuff to my bed."

"I certainly hope not."

"So what do you think?"

"About what?" she asked vaguely.

"About us, Violet." He was starting to get impatient again. For a smart woman, she certainly took her sweet time with some obvious things.

She exhaled. "You can't love me." Setting down her sandwich, she fixed him with her most level, nononsense gaze. Some men might've been intimidated by that. But Cooper had grown up with Yvonne Calhoun. Violet's quelling stare didn't even come close.

"Why can't I love you?" he challenged. "Do you have a reason?"

There were spots of hot color on her pale cheeks. "You can't possibly love me after I lied to you about Toni."

"I lied to you about Toni, too," he countered.

"Not about something as important as her being

my sister." Rising from her chair, Violet began to pace around his small kitchen. "It was just wrong of me not to tell you, and I don't see how you could ever trust me again."

"Because I see what's in your heart. How could I not trust you?" Cooper left the table, too, cornering Violet near the sink and making her look at him. He slipped his hands up into her hair, framing her face. "Kiss me, Violet," he murmured. "See how you feel."

He was convinced that she couldn't deny her feelings if she would just kiss him. There was plenty of heat between the two of them, every time they touched. But also heart. Violet was too honest. She would never be able to lie about that, not even to herself.

She hesitated, searching his face. In her eyes, those stormy lavender-blue eyes, he read fear and longing, but also hope. She licked her lip. "You really think you're in love with me?"

Holding her gaze, Cooper nodded, as serious as he'd ever been in his life. And Violet kissed him.

Stretching up, she pressed her lips to his, soft and sweetly expectant, testing him. He didn't want to freak her out, but he didn't have a whole lot of self-control when it came to her, so he just went with it. He kissed her back, deep and hot and hard, trying to tell her everything he felt with that one kiss, pouring himself into Violet.

After a long moment and one hell of a kiss, she broke away, gasping for oxygen. But she was smiling.

"I give up," she whispered. "I love you, too, Cooper. I can't believe it."

"I can."

Violet was thinking out loud, mulling it over, and he enjoyed the glimpse into how her brain worked. "The physical part of it is amazing, and that confused me. I was thinking it was just lust or frustrated libido or something."

"Well, that, too," he noted dryly.

She shook her head. "But there's more here. More between us. The thing is, I really like you." That made her laugh.

Cooper grinned. "That's a good thing."

"Uh-huh. I had fun with you. More fun than I've ever had in my entire life." She threw her arms around him, kissing him quickly. "And I, well, I trust you. You have the best heart and you're so loyal and honest and... I think you're the best man I ever met."

He wasn't sure about some of that, but he wasn't going to contradict her now.

Positively giddy, she nodded her head up and down, getting excited as she gained momentum. "I am crazy in love with you, Cooper. I didn't know. But I am!"

"That's all I need to hear," he murmured, reeling her in. "I love you like crazy. And I just want you to know, whether it takes handcuffs or leg irons or a ball and chain, I'm going to do my best to keep you in my life."

A little dubious, Violet allowed, "Handcuffs, okay. The rest of it...well, you may have to warm me up."

"I can do that."

"You," she teased, poking him in the ribs, "can do anything. As long as you're doing it with me."

_____Epilogue_____

TAKING A GANDER at the bumper crop around her dining room table, Yvonne Calhoun smiled, awfully pleased with how well things had turned out in such a short time. Eight people around her table for New Year's Day dinner, and another little one napping upstairs. All three sons matched up, and to the most interesting women. It was unbelievable, and absolutely wonderful.

And even her husband, crusty old Mike, had gotten into the spirit of things. Ever since that ghastly Toni blackmailing business, Mike had really seen the error of his ways. Keeping secrets from his wife? Not a good idea. Why, he had suddenly gotten positively romantic and affectionate in his old age.

"I showed him," Yvonne said under her breath as she set out another bottle of wine.

"What did you say, hon?" her husband asked, giving her a squeeze as she traipsed by.

Aw, isn't he sweet? She beamed down at her taciturn husband, happily kissing him on the top of his head. And he didn't even look embarrassed to be kissed in front of the kids, bless his heart.

"I just wanted to make a toast," she said, wrapping an arm around him and hefting her wineglass with the other hand. "First, to Holly, our brand-new granddaughter, the most gorgeous thing ever in the city of Chicago."

Everybody raised their glasses for that one, including the new parents, who were sitting very close together at the foot of the table, inches from the baby monitor.

"And then," Yvonne continued, "to the new First Deputy Superintendent of the Chicago Police Department, my husband, Michael Calhoun. No scandal can keep down a True Blue Calhoun! You beat the rap, Mike, you got the promotion and we all love you for it."

"You deserve the promotion, Dad. Nobody better," oldest son Jake ventured. "While I'm sorry I didn't find Toni for you and keep a lid on that whole thing, I'm not sorry with what I *did* find."

He winked at his girlfriend, that adorable little redhead, Zoë. She sat between him and his dad, smiling happily but not saying much. Yvonne could tell she was keeping a low profile, trying to be quiet and demure in these family surroundings. It wasn't easy for a girl in a sparkly reindeer sweatshirt and earrings that lit up like Christmas lights to keep a low profile, but Zoë was trying.

Mrs. Calhoun frowned. How many times was she going to have to tell that girl that the reason she was so perfect for Jake was because she was irreverent, mouthy and a breath of fresh air? Why, Jake was happier than he had ever been, and much less of a clone of his buttoned-up father. All because of Zoë, and all to the good as far as his mother was concerned. Zoë did fine with her sisters-in-law—they had bonded faster than the speed of light, as different as they were—but around the Calhoun men, she was a little quieter. Hmm... Yvonne made a mental note to work on opening up Zoë around the men. And, of course, she still needed to get the two of them married.

Sometimes it was good that Zoë was a free spirit, and sometimes not so good. Like on the subject of holy matrimony.

"Zoë, sweetheart," Yvonne began, moving around the corner to slide an arm around both her oldest son and his girlfriend, "are you ever going to say yes to poor Jake and put him out of his misery?"

"Ma, don't give Zoë a hard time about the *M* word." Jake broke in immediately. "She'll marry me when she's ready."

"He has to do the Explorer's Journey with me for real," Zoë stated. Her grin looked more spontaneous now, as she reached over and took Jake's hand. "That's my bottom line. And I'm not budging."

"That's all that's holding you back?" Mrs. Calhoun demanded. "That's it?"

"We're negotiating," Jake stated.

"No, we're not," Zoë retorted.

"Yes, we are."

"No—"

"Don't wait too long," Cooper said slyly from the other side of the table. "Sean and Abra have a jump start on you. Married, baby... They're making the rest of us look bad."

"Coop, don't say that in front of Zoë," Jake complained. "I don't want to freak her out by adding kids to this mix. I just want her to marry me first."

"Jake, face it—you're behind," Cooper teased. "Sean wins this one. Wife, kid. You can't even convince Zoë to get engaged."

"Hey, I got her onto the force, didn't I? One more True Blue Calhoun."

"Her name's not even Calhoun yet," Cooper argued. "That doesn't count. You have to have more Calhouns the old-fashioned way—give birth to them."

Jake picked up a dinner roll and pretended he was going to chuck it across the table at his brother, just as his mother plucked it out of his hand. She'd had enough food fights with these children when they were young, and she wasn't going to risk another one now.

"You are not messing up my nice dinner party," she said with righteous indignation. "What will the girls think—that I raised a bunch of heathens?"

"Don't you think the fact that Sean's already given Ma a grandchild means the rest of us are off the hook?" Jake continued, ignoring his mother. "Sean? Hey, bro, Holly will grow up True Blue, don't you think?"

"The kid's not even a month old and you're already making her a cop?" Cooper hooted.

"Why not?" their father interrupted, lowering his brows and looking stern.

"Mike," Yvonne warned, but he continued, anyway.

"What's wrong with that?" the Calhoun patriarch demanded. "Sean already said Holly could be a cop. And why not?"

Cooper raised an eyebrow. "Really? Sean, you said that?"

But his brother wasn't listening. Sean and his stunning blond wife, Abra, the former TV star, were whispering and holding hands down there, kissing, touching.... Oh, my.

Weren't they sweet? Yvonne started to get all misty. The poor things hadn't had any sleep in a month, ever since the baby came, and yet they still couldn't keep their eyes off each other. Their baby, christened Holloway Anna Calhoun and called Holly for short, was napping in the bedroom, in a brand-new crib Mrs. Calhoun had purchased just for the occasion. Such a perfect and beautiful couple, and such a gorgeous baby, who looked a great deal like her mother. A girl! After three boys, Yvonne was looking forward to this little girl. And to think that she herself, Yvonne Calhoun, had had a part in Sean and Abra finding each other.

If she hadn't thought her husband was having an affair, if she hadn't sent Sean looking for the wrong woman, why, Sean and Abra would never have gotten together. And look how wonderfully they fit. Sean kissed his wife tenderly, she gazed into his eyes and Mrs. Calhoun wanted to weep with the perfection of it.

"Hey, you guys, stop with all the mushy stuff down there. It's dinner."

Yvonne glared at Cooper. She wanted to thump him on the head, but she refrained, it being a holiday and all. "You leave Sean alone," she said darkly. "Abra, honey, don't listen to Cooper."

"What?" Abra looked up guiltily at the sound of her own name. "Did you say something, Mrs. Calhoun?"

"Call me Yvonne," she said for the four hundredth time. It was very strange having a daughter-in-law as polished and altogether perfect as Abra, even though she was really very sweet. But someone at her table who knew all those etiquette rules, who'd had dinner at the White House, and was now married to her Sean... Who'd ever have thought that was possible?

After they had managed a quiet wedding last August—*quiet* being the operative word and something everyone in the world thought was impossible for that tabloid twosome—Sean and Abra had set up house together in Chicago. Yvonne knew they were considering their options for the future, with Abra planning to go back to school and get the psychology degree she'd missed the first time around. Nearby Northwestern University was the front-runner, and Mrs. Calhoun was holding her breath it worked out so she could keep her new granddaughter close by. She had really fallen for that baby, hook, line and sinker.

"Hmm..." Should she go sneak a peek at the baby, just make sure she was okay? Not a peep from the baby monitor, but a quick check couldn't hurt....

But out of the blue, Violet, Yvonne's youngest son's girlfriend, piped up. "Anybody have any announcements to make?"

Mrs. Calhoun peered at Violet and Cooper, who looked suspiciously innocent over there. Neither one of them had said much all day, and that was definitely strange for Cooper.

It wasn't strange for Violet, but still... Yvonne narrowed her eyes, considering. She hadn't gotten a handle on Violet yet. She felt sure that part of the reason Violet was a little distant was that whole Toni business. After all, the girl who had caused them all so much trouble was her delinquent half sister, and poor Violet couldn't help but be sensitive about it. Yvonne figured she would just have to keep assuring Violet she did not hold the odious Toni against her. As long as Toni was not invited to the wedding or any family dinners, Mrs. Calhoun was good with the whole thing.

But Violet... Who was she? Smart, for sure, and feisty. Nuts about Cooper. That, too, was a certainty. And he was nuts about her right back. But where Zoë and Jake were always driving each other crazy, laughing and teasing and challenging, and Sean and Abra were so in love with each other and their baby that it took your breath away, Violet and Cooper were...different.

Yvonne had never seen her youngest son so settled.

That was it: settled. With Violet, Cooper suddenly seemed like a man. Out from under the shadow of his brothers, he seemed mature and strong and all grown up. A force to be reckoned with. And he and Violet together were the perfect team, as if the two pieces fitted together were stronger and more solid than either apart.

So why had they been putting their heads together all day, whispering and grinning like that?

She didn't see any point in beating around the bush. Flat out, she asked, "Okay, what's up with you two?"

"Yeah, Ma's right. You two have seemed weird today," Sean noted.

Everybody knew Sean was practically psychic. If he thought Cooper and Violet were acting oddly, something was definitely up.

"You were asking if anybody had any announcements. Why? Are you the ones with the announcement?" Mrs. Calhoun probed.

If it was another baby, she was hoping for some wedlock first this time. Nothing wrong with Sean and Abra tying the knot with the baby on the way, their circumstances being different, but she hoped Cooper and Violet wouldn't jump the gun and put the conception before the marriage.

"Well..." Violet smiled at Cooper. "Maybe you should go first."

"We got married yesterday," he said suddenly.

There was a hubbub of happy sounds, as both Abra

and Zoë jumped up to give Violet a squeeze and his brothers congratulated Cooper.

But Mrs. Calhoun was aghast. "What? No ring?"

"Violet didn't want—"

"She might've if you'd bought her one!" she shouted. "Cooper, where is your brain?"

"I swear, Ma, she said she didn't—"

But Yvonne wasn't done. "And you didn't invite us? You didn't let me put on a wedding for you?" She shook her head. She'd really thought she'd raised him better than that. "Sean and Abra sneaked away to Hawaii, which I understood because of all of those crazy press people, but now you two...? Am I ever going to get a decent wedding out of my children?"

She couldn't help but notice that Jake and Zoë both groaned. Darn tootin'. They were her last chance, and there was no way they were going to escape.

"Listen to me," she told them fiercely. "It might be a wedding where everybody throws tea leaves and a reception where you toast with carrot juice instead of champagne, but there is going to be a wedding, darn it!"

"You don't throw tea leaves, just read them," Zoë said helpfully. "And I like champagne." She came back around to stand next to Jake. "What do you think, Jake? How does June sound?"

His sharp intake of breath told everyone at the table what he thought. "Way too traditional for you," he said at first, but he followed it up with a hard, fast kiss, right there at the table.

Oh, there was definitely passion in that relationship, especially when Jake got rolling.

"Okay then. We'll plan for June." Mrs. Calhoun was already making mental notes about what needed to happen before then. The opportunity to plan Jake and Zoë's nuptials had her somewhat mollified. But not completely. Pointing at Cooper, she added, "Which doesn't let you off the hook."

"We had to do it quickly, because..." Cooper paused. "That's the other part of our announcement. I applied for FBI training at Quantico. And I was accepted."

"Coop, that's great," his dad said gruffly, as both brothers chorused good wishes.

"Oh, my heavens. Cooper, my baby, married. And an FBI agent!" Yvonne declared. "It's all so wonderful."

She ran around the table and gave Violet a quick hug.

"Why is everybody hugging her? I got married, too, and I'm the one who got into the academy."

"Yes, I know, but Violet is the one who got you to wake up and smell the coffee." She hugged her daughter-in-law again for good measure. "I'm not sure I can stand this much happiness. Wait till I tell Bebe!"

"Good old Bebe," Violet said with a laugh. She had her hair cut shoulder-length now, with her braid long gone. A Bebe special. And it looked so much better with all those soft curls free to tumble around her beautiful face.

"She said you have great hair," Abra interjected. "It looks beautiful, Vi."

"You think?" Violet crinkled up her nose, playing with a tendril near her face. "I wasn't sure, but..."

"I love it," Zoë volunteered. "I'm used to just chopping off my own hair with a scissors, but even I'm going to Bebe now. She's adding more space, because she's going to be doing manicures and pedicures and massages out of her salon, too."

"Really? My feet are a mess. I could definitely use a pedicure," Abra chimed in.

"And I may start reading tarot cards there." Zoë blushed, with hot pink color flooding her face all the way to the roots of her bright red hair. "Don't worry, Jake. I'm not taking it seriously. Just for fun. And for free."

Jake just shook his head. "Zo, you do whatever you want with your cards. I'm not going to fight it."

Yvonne wasn't used to having so many girls around, and having the dinner table conversation turn to hair and hot rollers and the best kind of pedicure seemed very odd. Calhouns were all more accustomed to discussing the latest search and seizure ruling around the table. As the voices rose and fell, each more lively than the next, she stepped back and just listened.

She still hadn't quite processed the information that Cooper was going to be an FBI agent. Jake, officially engaged to Zoë, both of them on the Chicago police force. Sean, married, a father, with his dazzling star wife set to be the psychologist she always should've been. And Cooper, married now, too, looking at a future of husband-and-wife Feds.

The True Blue Calhouns had always been the best sons a mother could ask for, but now... Seasoned by some terrific women, they were even better.

Yvonne Calhoun smiled at the chatter and disarray around her dinner table, enjoying every minute of it. Oh, she had plans. Wonderful plans. Once she got Jake and Zoë married, she could start pushing for more grandchildren. Holly would need some playmates.

And no matter how much her sons protested, their mother knew the truth. You could never have too many True Blue Calhouns.

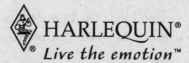

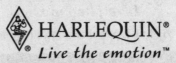

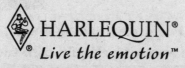

Let *USA TODAY* bestselling author JoAnn Ross
show you around Raintree, Georgia—steamy
capital of sin, scandal and murder....

JOANN ROSS

To her fans, Roxanne Scarbrough is the genteel
Southern queen of good taste—she's built an empire
around the how-to's of gracious living. To her critics—
and there are many—Roxanne is Queen Bitch. And
now somebody wants her dead.

SOUTHERN COMFORTS

"Ross delivers a sizzling, sensual romance sure to keep
hearts pounding."
—*Romantic Times* on *A Woman's Heart*

Available the first week of March 2004
wherever paperbacks are sold.

MIRA®